THE JONQUIL

Marilyn Parkes-Seddon

To Angela
from Marilyn
Jan 2019.

ARTHUR H. STOCKWELL LTD
Torrs Park, Ilfracombe, Devon, EX34 8BA
Established 1898
www.ahstockwell.co.uk

British Library Cataloguing-in-Publication Data.
A catalogue record for this book is available
from the British Library.

This is a work of fiction. Whilst most of the places mentioned in this
novel are genuine places in the Channel Islands, the yacht race, names,
characters and incidents are the product of the author's imagination
and any resemblance to actual persons, living or dead, is purely
coincidental.

ISBN 978-0-7223-4900-7
Printed in Great Britain by
Arthur H. Stockwell Ltd
Torrs Park   Ilfracombe
Devon EX34 8BA

DEDICATION

To Malc, the best husband in the world, and my greatest supporter. Also thank you to my friend, Angela, who persuaded me to send the book for publishing.

Chapter One

No one can deny it is a small island. Just three miles by one and a half miles, it hardly seems big enough to support a community, yet over 2,000 people live here. An island, windswept, with few trees, yet often bathed in an almost Mediterranean climate. Sitting looking out across the beach to the breakers on the sea wall, Betsy marvelled that she had come here to live.

So many people had told her it takes a lot of getting used to. Island life, they said, is not for everyone. Betsy had found this true, yet two months on she had no regrets as yet. This was Alderney, the least known of all the Channel Islands, but beautiful – Britain's little bit of France. It had proved her ideal escape. She hadn't intended leaving Wrenford after Tom died, but continued closeness to places and people which meant so much to both her and Tom had hindered the healing process.

"You need to get away, Betsy," her best friend, Katy, told her.

"Why? Will it make me feel any better?"

"It might, and you won't know unless you try it."

"But how can I go on holiday? It's the last thing I want. I'll be the opposite of the merry widow."

"I wasn't thinking of a holiday, Betsy."

And so here she was running the little harbour café and bistro for the summer season. Katy was right – she had needed to get away, and the Channel Islands were the perfect choice. Her grandfather had originally been from Guernsey, coming over to England in the war as a soldier – Joseph Deauville, and she had been Betsy Deauville before she married Tom. She would have space and time to sort herself out and also dig around looking for her family history at the same time. She knew little enough about it, and the Channel Islands themselves were somewhat of a mystery to her.

She was roused from her thoughts by Julie, the barmaid, arriving for work.

"Penny for them," Julie said. "You looked miles away."

"Oh, Julie, hi. You're early. I think I was a bit mesmerised by the waves. It's a bit rough out there today. You know, where I come from we're miles away from the sea. It's amazing to be so close. It becomes part of your life, doesn't it? The noise, the smell, the seabirds – so different."

"But do you like it?"

"Oh, I do, Julie, I do. It's so beautiful and peaceful here, but I have to admit it is quite hard getting used to island life."

"Especially a small island like this one, eh?" answered Julie.

"Listen – could you hold the fort here while I just nip into town? We're low on a few things."

"No problem – off you go. If you aren't back on time I'll open up."

"Great. Thanks, Julie. Do you want anything?"

"No, I don't think so, Betsy."

Yes, into town, and it wasn't a slip of the tongue. Despite the smallness of the island, Betsy had been totally surprised to find a perfect little town here, St Anne, with winding streets of tiny cottages painted in various pastel shades.

And sloping down from the top of the town the one main street leading down to the sea, with its assortment of shops catering for locals and visitors alike, though several shops catered especially for yachtsmen and women, who made up the majority of visitors. It was a popular place to sail to and stop off at, with the yacht club as an added bonus. The bistro too was popular with sailors, being the first stop after mooring up in the small harbour.

This was Saturday and Betsy set off up the main street. It was busy on a Saturday. It was a good time and place to meet people, as locals wandered up and down and in and out of the various small shops, continually greeting friends and neighbours, stopping to catch up on the local gossip. But Betsy didn't know many people yet, so she didn't expect to be held up by greetings and gossip, enabling her to quickly get what she needed and then head back down to the harbour. It was a lovely spring day, but walking back she noticed the breeze getting stronger. She had learnt that, subject to the offshore conditions, the weather could change rapidly. Heading into the wind, she was glad to reach the bistro, and noticed too the white horses showing on the sea as the weather looked set to turn.

"You were quick," said a surprised Julie.

"I know – I hurried up when I noticed the weather was on the turn. If it gets much rougher out there we won't get many yachts coming over for the weekend.

"No, it could be quiet, but we've got a few tables booked, so it shouldn't be too bad."

"Right, well, come on – let's get the show on the road, shall we?"

Betsy didn't have any plans for her day off on Sunday. That wasn't to say that there was nothing to do on the island (it was surprisingly rich with clubs and activities); it was just that she didn't really know anyone yet. And if she was really truthful, she didn't feel ready to socialise – not yet. She knew she should be over the grieving stage now – it was over eighteen months since Tom had died – but recovery was easier said than done; if willing herself to feel better was possible then she would have done it. It was just so hard. They had been so in love. It seemed so unfair then, and it still did. The suddenness hadn't helped. One minute Tom was there; the next he was dead. Yes, life is fragile – precious. They hadn't had enough time together, and he was so young. He'd had a massive brain haemorrhage. He was dead before he even got to hospital.

"There really was nothing we could do, Mrs Abbot. Even if we could have got him here sooner, he would still have died. The haemorrhage was large, devastating and fatal," the kind doctor had explained.

Her life was in pieces. She was coping better now, but she was far from recovered.

'Perhaps being here will help me. I hope so – I do so hope it will. I need to get over this, this terrible feeling, this permanent ache in my stomach, the panic and frightening feelings of dreadful loss.'

Allain Laubert loved his yacht, which was just as well because it consumed all of his free time and most of his money. And he knew it was worth it. As soon as he stepped on to the pontoon he felt his spirits rise. The anticipation of pleasure never diminished. Then as he sailed out from St Peter Port and entered the open sea the exhilaration transformed his face into one of wide smiles and obvious satisfaction with his life. For he was indeed happy with his life. A Guernsey man, as were his many ancestors, he was born and brought up on Guernsey. He loved it and never wanted to leave. He knew where he belonged. Allain worked in the finance industry, for which the Channel Islands are well known – a lucrative post, which gave him enjoyment, satisfaction and security.

Allain knew he was lucky. He had a great life and he enjoyed it to the full. And just now he was content with his single life; of course he was an eligible bachelor, but for the moment he had no time and little spare money to even wonder about whether he wanted a wife.

So, like most other Saturdays, Allain eased the *Jonquil* out of the harbour into the wide, expansive sea. Yet the weather was contrary and he knew the wind was rising. It wasn't promising, so he convinced himself he wouldn't stay out too long – be back before it became too rough. By the time he returned he had made up his mind to enter the St Anne Challenge, a yacht race to take place in August – a challenge consisting of a race three times around the island of Alderney. The race was held every two years and this would be his first time. Allain was confident his skills were sufficient – maybe not to win, but he'd certainly make a good effort. He knew that, yes, it is a small island, but a challenge it would certainly be; the tides were notoriously unpredictable and dangerous.

"I'll have to get some practice in," he told himself.

Back in the marina he bumped into a sailing friend.

"Robert, hi there. Are you going out or coming in? It's pretty rough today."

"It is," replied Robert. "I came back in myself just a while ago. Wouldn't want to go back out. How's the *Jonquil*? Is she sailing well?"

"Great, yes – in fact I've just decided I'm going to enter the Challenge around Alderney this year."

"Really? That's great, but it will be tough, you know. Say, tell you what, do you fancy a drink? You don't need to get off yet, do you?"

"No, no. Yes, that'd be great – time to catch up. Pub or clubhouse?"

"Pub's fine for me."

"Right, let's go, then," said Allain.

In the event, even without a plan, Sunday passed OK for Betsy. In the morning she went to church, where people were welcoming and friendly.

"How are you settling in?" one of the members asked over a cup of tea after the service.

"OK – good, thanks. The bistro is doing fine. It's still early in the season, so I expect it will gradually get busier. And I was so lucky to have the flat included with the job – such a perfect spot, although I must admit you can never get away from the sound of the sea. Trying to get to sleep can be difficult, on stormy nights especially."

"Yes, I know what you mean, but you'll find that when you move away it will seem strange without the familiar wash of the waves. I'm Barbara, by the way."

"Betsy – Betsy Abbot."

"And what made you come to Alderney, then, Betsy? It's a bit of a backwater."

"For personal reasons I needed to get away, and my grandfather was a Guernsey man. I've always wanted to come to the Channel Islands and see for myself where he lived. It seemed a perfect opportunity."

"You'll know some of our history, then," continued Barbara. "It's a lovely place now, but it's had its very dark days and so have the island people."

"I do know some of the history, of course," answered Betsy, "but I'd like to find out a lot more while I'm here. Anyway, lovely to meet you. I'm hoping to get some fresh air, do a little walking. Hope to see you again. Bye."

Betsy left, encouraged by the ease with which she had

coped with meeting Barbara. She was beginning to feel much more relaxed, settled even.

"I do believe it is doing me good to be here," she told herself.

Deciding to go straight on for a walk, she headed off up on to the cliff path. It was a blustery day, but with blue sky, and it was very clear. The air was clean and pure and refreshing. She really did know some of the history of the Channel Islands, especially about the German invasion during the Second World War. Alderney itself she knew had actually been evacuated, and the island became a slave labour camp, where German prisoners were expected to build endless fortifications. Hundreds died and are buried on the island. The population was higher then, and of the 4,000 people evacuated only 500 returned after the war.

Betsy enjoyed her solitary walk. The cliffs were empty, but she sat for what seemed like hours watching the hundreds of seabirds swooping, fishing and landing on the cliff ledges. It was a glorious sight. She returned more peaceful and optimistic than she had felt for a long time.

During the following week Allain was preoccupied with planning an initial visit to Alderney, hopefully on a good day. Of course he'd been before. He often completed longer sails, going also to the French coast and occasionally to Jersey too. But this time he felt his visit was purposeful – the start of the planning process for the race. He was excited at the prospect. On the Friday he was taking Francesca for a meal, then meeting up with other friends. He liked Francesca. He saw more of her than of any of the other women in his life, but both she and he knew there was no commitment on either side. Whether or not Francesca was truly happy with the arrangement he didn't know, but she knew where he stood.

She was a solicitor in St Peter Port and, like Allain, was

born and raised on Guernsey. On the Friday evening they sat on the restaurant's outside terrace by the sea waiting for their friends to arrive, the evening bright, the air still and the sea calm.

"So are you really entering the Challenge, then? asked Francesca.

"Definitely," Allain replied. "I feel confident and experienced enough. I have a good boat – she's fast and reliable. Plus I know Alderney, and by deciding now I'll have plenty of time to practise. I'm not saying I'll win, but I do think I'll finish, however rough it might get."

"You are determined."

"I am, Fran, but I'm so excited at the prospect of it. I can't wait. Oh, look – here are the others. Just in time, I'm starving. Come on – let's go and join them and go straight to our table."

"Perhaps we can come and sit outside later, Allain," suggested Francesca. "It's such a lovely evening – quite balmy and still."

"We'll do that. We could even move on somewhere else right by the water."

'That would be nice."

"I was wondering too if you'd like to come out on the yacht with me next Saturday. All being well, I'm sailing over to Alderney. We could have lunch in the bistro, on the harbour, and then have a few drinks in the club."

"That would be great. You know I'm not a great sailor though – if it's rough I'll stay on Guernsey."

"Fine, but you'll never improve if you don't persist, you know, but I understand. Be nice if you did come though."

"Anyway, come on – let's get to that table."

Betsy had a good if uneventful week. Le Chapeau was still quiet – it was very early in the season – but she was coping with the work and was getting along with Julie too, which was great. The weekends were likely to get busy as yachtsman were beginning their visits in the fine spring weather, and locals seemed to like the place too. It was small but cosy and informal, but its main asset was the outdoor terrace which overlooked the harbour on one side and the beach on the other. It was a perfect place to sit and watch the world go by, and the sunsets were beautiful.

Betsy knew that over the next couple of weeks she would need to think about working on Sundays too. Julie and the chef couldn't manage between them, but on Monday the bistro was closed so that would still give her one day off. She had still not managed to see the island; she would have to make a concerted effort soon. She told Julie the same thing.

Julie replied, "Well, what are you doing on Sunday morning? There is a little guided walk – it'll only last a couple of hours. I'm sure you'd enjoy it. You'll see around the town and out to the coast; you'll learn a bit about our history too. Why don't you go?"

"That would be nice, wouldn't it? But I'll make sure I'm back to open up here."

"Don't worry about it – I can manage. We aren't that busy yet, are we?"

"I will, then. Thanks, Julie."

The following Saturday dawned bright and beautiful, a perfectly calm, warm day. Quite a few people had come for late lunch, sitting on the terrace soaking up the sunshine. They were all enjoying themselves, chatter and laughter all around. Behind the bar Betsy watched as a man and his girlfriend walked in. She was astonished at her reaction to him, his immediate charisma, confidence and energy. He was handsome too in the rugged sailorly sort of way. Here was a man used to getting his own way, satisfied with life and enjoying it to the full. His light hair was tousled, not long, but with soft curls just touching the collar of his jacket. His girlfriend too was beautiful, and yet in comparison with his charisma she faded into the background.

"Simon," he shouted to a man stood by the bar, "how are you?"

"Hello, Allain. Didn't expect you here today. I'm well – you too, I take it?"

"Oh, yes, great. Simon, not sure if you've met, but this is Francesca. She sailed over from Guernsey with me. Wouldn't have come if it hadn't been so calm though, would you, darling?"

"No," answered Francesca, "I'm not such an accomplished sailor as you. I'm getting better though. Anyway, Simon, pleased to meet you."

"So no Annabel with you today?" asked Allain of Simon's wife.

"No, she decided to stay and get a bit of retail therapy."

"What are you drinking, then? Can I get you a drink?" Allain asked.

"Thanks. Yes, a pint of shandy would be great."

"Fine, and G & T for you, Fran?"

"Oh, please. Thanks."

Allain approached the bar and Betsy went over to serve him.

"What can I get you, sir?" she said.

"A pint of shandy, a G & T and a small whisky, please. Now, I haven't seen you here before. Are you the new barmaid?"

"I'm the new manager, Betsy Abbot. I agreed to stay here for the season. Nice to meet you."

"Well, I'm Allain. This is my friend Simon and this is Francesca. We've sailed over from Guernsey."

14

"Have you?" replied Betsy. "Do you often come over?"

"Quite often. I like Alderney, and the sail from Guernsey is a challenge. But I'm likely to be over more often this year – I'm entering the Challenge."

"Oh," answered Betsy, a little perplexed. "What's the Challenge?"

"Now, we can tell you aren't local or you would know. It's famous here. The Challenge is a biennial yacht race, three times around the island. Never done it before myself, but I'm looking forward to my first attempt."

"So you're going to do a lot of practising, then," said Simon.

"I'll need to, won't I?" laughed Allain. "So," said Allain, addressing Betsy again, "there must be a lot more about Alderney still to learn."

"I dare say. I've only been here a couple of months and don't know many people."

"So do you know about the albino hedgehogs and the wild black rabbits?"

"I have heard of them, yes, but haven't seen any yet though."

"Then what about the Alderney cows?" continued Allain.

"Haven't heard of them, no. Is there really an Alderney cow? Are they not the same as Guernseys?"

"On no, don't let the locals hear you say that. They are similar, but much lighter coloured with long black ears."

"Oh, right. Anyway, here are your drinks."

"Thanks. We'll take them outside. Don't forget to look for the cows."

They left, Allain full of amusement, and Betsy saw them take a table on the terrace.

'He seemed so friendly,' she said to herself, 'so easy-going and relaxed.' She noticed too that his green eyes had sparkled with pleasure and amusement, and she felt disconcerted at the effect he had on her. Which was what? She didn't quite know. Not that she had time to really think about it – the lovely day had brought people out. It was busy and the terrace was sparkling with sunshine and the laughter of the customers. Betsy conceded it was a good day.

Betsy struggled to get up on Sunday morning. She felt jaded. The bistro had had its busiest day on the Saturday and Betsy had been worn out. She couldn't wait to have a hot bath and then go straight to bed after closing time. She fell asleep immediately. Whatever the weather was it wouldn't have kept her awake.

'I'm sure I won't always be so tired after a busy day. Hope not anyway – couldn't cope with it. It's just getting used to it. I'll be fine,' she convinced herself. She had a lazy breakfast, taking it out on to the balcony overlooking the beach. It was chilly. The weather was deceiving. 'It's still only early spring,' she told herself. 'The mornings and evenings can still be cold. Even so it promises to be a lovely day, I think.' Lost in her own thoughts she finally managed to rouse herself, noticing how cold she felt. 'I'm not sure I really want to go on the walk,' she told herself as she moved back inside, 'but what would I tell Julie? She'll think I'm a right wimp. No, I'll go – I'll enjoy it when I get there.'

There were only eight people for the walk, and that was fine by Betsy – less overwhelming. The guide introduced himself as Jules, the islands' conservation officer. The others introduced themselves and Betsy learnt that two were locals, two were weekenders from Jersey, and three others were a family on holiday.

"We'll walk all the way," explained Jules. "But don't worry, it isn't far – nowhere is far on Alderney."

And everyone laughed.

"It may not be far, but we'll see lots of interesting things, historical and natural, so I hope you will enjoy the walk. Let's go."

It was quite easy walking, often on roads and sometimes on springy grass, and Betsy started to enjoy herself. They went to the lighthouse first and then Jules explained about the forts all around the island. Many were German, but quite a few were built at the time of the Napoleonic Wars, the Channel Islands being of strategic importance. But the reminders of the German occupation were a sad, grim sight. A huge lookout tower called the Odeon still stood strong, intimidating and incongruous, surrounded by heath and dunes, and Betsy saw pyramid orchids growing all around. It was unpleasantly atmospheric and she didn't like it.

"Now as we head back we'll call at the campsite. The owner knows we are coming, and there'll be tea and coffee there for us."

"That will be welcome," the holiday family said to Betsy. "It may not have been a long walk, but it's still tiring."

"You're right, it is," replied Betsy. "I'll be glad to sit down for a moment."

The campsite was small, but sheltered between high sand dunes, a flat area sandwiched between. As they sat at the little outdoor café, Betsy was content to let the sun beat on her face.

'So sheltered. You could really get a tan here,' she told herself.

"Now," said Jules, quietening them down, "it seems very peaceful here, but the reality is that this is the actual spot of the slave labour camp, where so many prisoners lived and also died. It's hard to believe now, but on less sunny, cheerful days this place has a very strange atmosphere. Am I right, Albert?" he shouted to the site owner.

"Dead right," he answered. "It's very weird sometimes, ominous and sad."

"Anyway, when you've finished we'll head back."

As they set off Betsy walked at Jules' side.

"Are we likely to see any Alderney cows on the way back, or nearby?" asked Betsy.

"Pardon?" And she thought Jules was going to choke. "What made you ask that?"

"Well, I was told I might see them on the island."

"Whoever told you that was having you on, love. There are no Alderney cows. There did used to be, but they've been extinct for well over 100 years. The only ones you'll see are in a photo in the museum." And he laughed. He approached the other walkers. "Betsy wants to know if we'll see any Alderney cows on the walk. What do you think?"

"She'll be lucky," replied one of the Alderney residents.

"She can come and see some Jersey cows on my brother's farm," said another.

"Leave her alone," pleaded one of the visitors. "You've really embarrassed her. She can't see the joke."

Betsy felt her cheeks hot with embarrassment and felt tears pricking her eyes. No, she couldn't see the joke, especially when the joke was on her.

'Allain – how could he! He was deliberately mocking me, making fun. I'll never live this down. Oh, why did I come? Why? I thought he seemed so nice, but he was just arrogant – full of himself.' Betsy couldn't stop the tears. She felt so lonely, so alone.

Chapter Two

Betsy didn't tell anyone about her embarrassing faux pas, but she couldn't forget it. For days afterwards the whole experience would come back to her. It was as if her whole life on Alderney had become sullied. It took all her willpower not to just pack up and go home, she felt so miserable. 'This wasn't how my life was supposed to be', she said to herself. 'If Tom were here my life would be so different, so happy, so contented. How will I ever get a decent life back?' Her future seemed to stretch before her bleak and unhappy. She felt so homesick and the slightest thing would bring tears and grief and regret.

Perhaps she shouldn't have come – it was too far from where she felt safe. But on telephoning her best friend, Katy, she felt comforted, especially when Katy promised to visit.

"Will you really come, Katy? Oh, it would be so lovely. Oh, I do so want to see you."

"Betsy, of course I'll come. If me coming will help you stay put instead of getting the first plane home, then try and stop me. And anyway, I can't wait to see where you're living and eye up some of these sailors you keep mentioning."

"I'll look forward to it. Perhaps we could go over to Guernsey too. When do you think you could come?"

"Soonish, but let me plan some leave and organise things.

Sometime in the next two or three weeks should be possible."

"OK, but make it as soon as you can, please."

The thought of Katy coming over lifted Betsy's mood, and planning her visit gave her something to think about other than work. Yet she was getting used to the bistro and its regular customers. She couldn't say she had made any friends, but the customers and locals alike were always friendly and kind. Betsy knew it was a really good place to be and she was determined to try her best to look forward to the rest of the season with something like optimism and even pleasure.

Many of the yachtsmen were regular visitors to the island, where they enjoyed their time off, and the bistro, particularly at weekends, could be rowdy and boisterous, though always good-natured. They were a mixture of people, all with the same fascination with yachts and the sea, but they were interesting and Betsy enjoyed talking to them and learning where they came from and what they did. And she was relieved that since their first encounter Allain had not been back to the bistro. Betsy didn't know how she would handle it if he did. But of course she knew it was inevitable that he would reappear at some point. It could be just days or even weeks ahead, but she knew arrive he would. So it wasn't unexpected when one dull but calm Saturday towards the end of April he came into the bistro. When Betsy saw him, he was laughing, sharing a joke with a fellow yachtsman. Betsy immediately dashed into the kitchen to think. Fortunately the bistro was busy so she had an excuse to be bustling about, which she hoped meant she could ignore him. She calmed herself and re-entered. He was standing by the bar, Julie serving him drinks, and he walked off with the menu. She felt her stomach lurch as she realised he was eating as well as drinking and wouldn't be going for a while. She watched him find a table, and then with his friend, whom she hadn't seen in Le Chapeau before, he was deep in conversation. Francesca wasn't with him this weekend. Allain must have sensed her eyes on him. He looked at her, amusement sparkling in his beautiful eyes. Was he laughing at her, mocking her, again?

"Betsy, hi," he shouted over to her. "Are you settled in now?"

"Yes, I'm fine, thank you." She forced herself to walk across to him. "Are you ready to order?"

"I am; are you, Robert?" he asked his companion, who nodded.

Betsy felt herself starting to sweat.

"I'll get Julie to come and take your order, then."

She almost ran over to Julie to ask her to take over. Stupidly and unexpectedly Betsy felt tears pricking her eyes. 'I need to get out. I just can't stay in here,' she said to herself. 'What is wrong with me? How stupid can I be?'

"What's wrong with her? Was it something I said?" questioned Allain of Robert.

She approached Julie as she was heading to the kitchen. She said, "Julie, I'm just nipping out to the shops. I need a bit of fresh air. I won't be long."

"Are you OK?" asked Julie, concerned.

"Yes, I'm fine. I'll see you later."

"You don't look fine. Take care. Go and have a stroll – I can cope here."

Betsy had to pass Allain on her way out.

"Hey, you OK there?" he asked. "You don't look too well."

"I'm fine, thank you," she replied somewhat aggressively, and hurriedly went out.

She caught sight of him as she walked away. He looked genuinely concerned, and she was surprised.

Betsy sat on a bench a little distance away facing the

beach and immediately felt better. 'Idiot,' she chastised herself. 'What is wrong with you? You're a grown woman. He was just joking with you. He didn't know I was miserable and cross with him; nor did he know how I made a fool of myself on the walk. And he did look really worried about me. But it's his fault I was upset in the first place, isn't it,' she countered, 'with his silly joke? Stupid man!'

Allain felt somehow disappointed and didn't enjoy his lunch as much as he had expected. He knew he gave the appearance of being a hale fellow well met, a man of great jokes and casual chatter. Yet looks could be deceiving. Underneath, Allain was far more perceptive and sensitive, he just didn't like to show it. Somehow it didn't quite go with the image he'd created for himself. Yet he didn't always like his own image, he admitted to himself. He was sure that Betsy had been deliberately ignoring him and he didn't know why. He was also sure she was very upset about something and was finding it hard to keep her emotions under control. And he didn't know why that was either.

"Hey, you seem a bit deep in thought, Allain?" questioned Robert, surprised that his upbeat mood seemed to have disappeared.

"No, no, don't worry – I'm fine really. It's just that the new manager seems to have taken a dislike to me. Can't think why. I don't know her – haven't even spoken to her hardly. It's ridiculous. She needs to be careful – she can't go around treating her customer like that. Anyway, I'm not going to let that bother me. Come on – let's drink up, eat up and go and find somewhere a bit more sociable."

But despite his words and forced good humour, Allain still felt unaccountably unsettled. They left and as they were walking towards the yacht club he noticed Betsy sitting by the beach and took a deliberate wide circle around her to avoid her and keep her from seeing him.

Betsy did see him though, even if only out of the corner of her eye. Again her stomach clenched, but knowing he had left the bistro she got up and walked back.

"There you are," welcomed Julie. "You look better."

"I am, thanks. I don't know what came over me. Thanks for holding the fort. Have you coped?"

"'Course I have, but now you're back I think I'll have a break and a cup of tea."

Betsy did feel better, very relieved that Allain had gone. 'Why did he make me feel like that? Forget it, Betsy. He's not a nice man – he doesn't matter.'

Yet, despite what she told herself, if she was honest, she knew that he did matter. For some reason his impressions of her mattered very much.

'But please don't come back too soon. Life will be so much easier and calmer without this feeling of embarrassment, and continual tears. Give me the space to get on with my new life. Please.'

Still feeling irritated, Allain and Robert took refuge in the yacht club, where Allain was pleased to see many of his acquaintances enjoying a drink and chatting good-humouredly. He decided too to check on the list of applications for the yacht race. The club captain was able to give him an approximate list and he was surprised that even at this early stage about thirty sailors had already registered. He wandered back to Robert.

"Not good news, Robert. There is going to be some very strong competition here. Perhaps I'm being a bit overconfident in thinking I can compete with them. There are so many really experienced competitors, I don't think I have a chance."

Robert scanned down the list Allain gave him. He was right: he wasn't going to find it easy at all.

"Allain, you knew it would be difficult, but don't be defeatist. You have to start somewhere, and what's more you are a skilled yachtsman, just as good as most of these. They may have had more experience, but you are equally good."

"Oh, I don't know, Robert. I'm getting cold feet, I think. I don't want to make an idiot of myself, and I'm not the equal of most of these."

"And why would you do that? You may not win, but you'll finish, I'm sure you will, and for a first-timer that is some accolade, really it is. It's a tough challenge, but you can do it."

"Do you really think so?" asked Allain unconvincingly.

"'Course you can. What's happened to you? You seem so down – it's not like you."

"No, I know. I just wonder if I've bitten off more than I can chew. And the practice will take all my spare time."

"So, what's new!" exclaimed Robert.

"You're right, of course," smiled Allain. "Of course I can do it."

Underneath Allain no longer felt confident, but his determination kicked in and he knew he wouldn't back out.

"I'm going to give it everything I've got," he said. And his spirits lifted.

"Should think so!" commented Robert. "Now come on – let's get that drink. I think we both need one."

"You're right," agreed Allain. "These are on me."

He sailed back home the following morning, feeling much more determined. There was a stiff breeze, he felt exhilarated and he had completely forgotten the tearful manager of the bistro – or at least he thought he had. He had phoned Francesca from Alderney. She was pleased to hear from him and he was determined to enjoy her company on his return, and to show off his new-found confidence to his colleagues at the marina. He would give his competitors something to think about.

Meanwhile Betsy was preparing for another day at work. Saturdays had been really busy and she had realised that she was going to need more staff at the weekend, as the season built up. She would have to look at recruiting someone this week. Yet she knew she had been glad to be busy. It had taken her mind off Allain, and when she finally went to bed, feet aching, head buzzing, she fell into a deep sleep. In fact Sunday wasn't so hectic as she had anticipated. The morning's crisp air and fresh breeze changed at lunchtime into dark clouds, then sleety rain which stung the skin, and which lasted most of the afternoon. Early diners quickly went back home, yachtsmen set off earlier to avoid worsening weather, and those contemplating going out changed their minds and stayed in, perhaps watching TV instead. On a rainy day Alderney, like other seaside places in rough weather, could be miserable and depressing and Betsy hoped that the finer spring weather would soon return.

And the weather did warm, and over the next couple of weeks customers came and went. The bistro was doing well; it was becoming part of Betsy's life. The local beaches were never crowded, but local families and visitors alike enjoyed them, and Betsy could hear their laughter, screams and splashes as the noises wafted up from the beach to her bar and terrace. There seemed no nicer thing to do than sit out there with a drink or food, or both, watching the world go by – a bit of people-watching, seeing them enjoying themselves.

'What could be nicer', she said to herself, realising a change had come over her, 'than living and working in a place that is able to provide such pleasure and happiness?' She felt satisfied and relaxed – more than she had felt for months. Also Katy, her friend, was arriving in a few days' time. Betsy had arranged to take a few days off and she was so looking forward to spending some time exploring and being with her friend. She had also booked a short break in Guernsey, where she hadn't yet been and which she very much wanted to see.

There was no ferry to Alderney from anywhere, so all visitors and locals coming and going to many different places had no choice but to fly. Betsy smiled as she greeted Katy at the tiny island airport. She knew what the look of shock and the pale skin meant. She recognised the sickly look and Katy's shocked expression as she approached Betsy.

Betsy herself had felt the same when she first arrived, and she had selfishly not told Katy what to expect of the flight. She didn't want the reality of the small plane to put her off. She desperately wanted to see her and so wanted no obstacles whatsoever.

"You call that a plane!" exclaimed Katy as she walked towards Betsy, relief at being on the ground again showing clearly in her expression.

Betsy laughed. "Only way to get here, Katy, and it is so wonderful to see you." And she hugged her friend. "And it's lucky you flew on a calm day. When it's windy the plane has to land on the grass runway."

"Oh, don't, Betsy. I don't want to think about it. Oh, you look so well – it must be all this sea air."

"Come on – give me your case. Henry, my chef, has lent me his car so we don't need a taxi."

In just a few minutes they were in the centre of town. It was a lovely day and the town and island were looking their best.

"Oh, Betsy, what a lovely little town – so unexpected, so pretty and quaint. Where's your bistro? Is it in town?"

"Well, not exactly. It's just outside by the harbour. We're nearly there, and we can sit outside and have a drink and catch up with all your news. It's a perfect day for sitting and not doing a lot."

"That sounds great to me, Betsy."

Betsy parked the car outside, and while Katy got out she went through the bistro to tell Henry they were back. Then she went to get Katy's case.

"I'll take your case through. You sit on the terrace and I'll bring us both a drink. G & T OK?"

"Wonderful. Oh, Betsy, it's gorgeous. What a fantastic view – boats bobbing in the harbour and then the expanse of sand and shimmering sea. It's like the south of France – no wonder you like it here."

"Well, it's not quite Mediterranean; but yes, I suppose it is lovely."

The days flew by, and Betsy knew that having Katy to stay had proved the antidote to her homesickness and gave her back her confidence and tenacity to stay on Alderney. She knew going home to Wrenford would have signalled a failure and she wanted deeply to move on and find a new life for herself. They wandered into town, around the harbour, and walked on the beach, but mostly relaxed in bars and cafés, enjoying the companionship that comes with close friendship. Betsy was grateful to Katy – she was a very special friend.

"Thank you for coming, Katy," Betsy said as she reached across and took her hand. "I would have scurried back home, I'm sure, if you hadn't come."

"Don't be daft," laughed Katy. "It was no great sacrifice to come here. It's gorgeous. I really like it – apart from the plane, that is."

And they both laughed.

"Seriously though, Betsy, what went wrong? You haven't mentioned what happened to upset you."

"No, I know, and it doesn't matter now, honestly. I'm fine and, trying to explain, well, it just seems so silly now. You'd only laugh at me, and you would be right to."

But later in the quiet of the evening she did tell Katy about the Alderney cow and how she had been afraid to encounter Allain again. And Katy did laugh, but in a kind way, and both acknowledged that, no, it didn't matter any more.

"So we're off to Guernsey tomorrow," Betsy said to Katy. "I'm really looking forward to it, and you can help me look for my family's house."

"We don't have to go on that plane again, do we?"

"'Fraid so. There's no other way, so if you want to see Guernsey then plane it is."

"Oh, OK," groaned Katy.

As it was, it was a calm and cloudless day. Flying at less than 1,000 feet, the sea below was clear, shining in a myriad of colours, the occasional small boats heading between the islands.

"We seem so close, we can almost see what books they're reading and what they're drinking," Katy giggled, pleased that the flight was less frightening than previously.

You could hardly call Guernsey bustling, but after Alderney it almost seemed so. St Peter Port, the capital, was a beautiful town, the harbour and marina huge, with cruise liners lying offshore. There was so much to see and do, but with their time so limited both knew they wouldn't see much. Their hotel was close to a beach, but they had little time to laze, finding instead the pleasure of exploring St Peter Port, shopping, and generally enjoying themselves. At the end of the day they ate a quiet meal at the hotel – they were too tired to do anything else.

Bright and early next morning they set off again, taking a taxi into town. Betsy knew only a very little of her Guernsey family history, but she did have her grandfather's address and over a cup of mid-morning coffee they studied a street map and realised that the street was still there. Excited, they set off to find it, getting a little lost in the backstreets of the old town where her grandfather had lived.

"Look – there it is, Rue Normandie," Katy said. "What number did you say it was – 47?"

"Yes, 47 Rue Normandie, St Peter Port, I'm sure."

It was a lovely old cobbled street, and when looking down it there was a clear view to the sea. It was a sloping street with wide steps, and a little square at the bottom.

"I didn't expect anything like this!" exclaimed Betsy. "I didn't even expect it to still be here. It's so lovely. I wonder who lives at number 47 now?"

"Let's go and ask," Katy suggested, and set off towards it.

"No, I couldn't – not today, anyway. Maybe I'll write to the occupier and ask if I can visit another time."

"That's a good idea," agreed Katy.

"Oh, Katy," I feel a bit emotional.

"Come on, softy – let's go and find a café. It's lunchtime."

And they set off down the street with its wide steps emerging near the harbour, where a little further on was an open-air café, perfect for a lazy lunch.

They both chose crab salad and a glass of chilled white wine. Both felt relaxed and in no hurry to leave; they watched the boats in the harbour, saw people heading out to visit Castle Cornet and generally enjoyed being part of the town's hustle and bustle.

Not expecting anyone to speak to her, Betsy jumped when she heard her name. She turned to see who had spoken and a prepared smile froze on her face. She put on her sunglasses to hide her emotions. It was Allain Laubert and he had seemingly just come into the café.

"It is Betsy Abbot, from the Alderney bistro, isn't it? Or have I made a mistake? In which case I apologise."

"No, you're right," came Betsy's icy reply. "Yes, I am Betsy Abbot."

"Right, well, I just wanted to say hello – perhaps see you in the bistro again?"

"Maybe," Betsy replied coldly.

She turned round, away from him, as he moved and sat down at a table a little distance from them.

"Betsy, what was all that about? It isn't like you to be so rude. You embarrassed and upset him. He's absolutely drop-dead gorgeous. Why did you snub him?"

"Because he upset me and embarrassed me too. That's Allain Laubert, who sent me on the wild goose chase over the cows. I didn't know what to say to him anyway."

"Well, he obviously wanted to speak to you, yet you never gave him a chance."

"I know. Well, it's too late now. Come on – drink up and we'll go."

As they were about to leave, Allain came over to them again.

"I'm sorry to ask this," he said nervously, "but have I done or said something to upset you? I can't understand why you are so brusque. What is it? If you tell me I can apologise, but I don't know what I've done."

"Don't you?" replied Betsy fiercely. "Well, it is probably nothing to you, but you must have thought it very funny to make fun of me in front of your and my friends. Is that how you get your fun? Sad really."

"Will you tell me what you are talking about, because I have absolutely no idea?"

"Telling me to look for the Alderney cows. I know I'm gullible and your friends had a good laugh, and so did the people on the walk when I asked the guide to show me any Alderney cows!"

Betsy heard Katy giggle, and Allain too was finding it hard not to burst out laughing.

"What's so funny!"

"Betsy," said Allain, now unable to refrain from smiling, "it was April the 1st. It was a joke. I didn't know you would believe it."

"Oh," said Betsy, now embarrassed all over again and feeling doubly stupid.

"But anyway I'm sorry – I shouldn't have said it. It was a silly thing to say."

Then Betsy too started to laugh. She knew the incident had indeed been both silly and unintended.

"I was just about to order coffee; would you both stay and have one too?"

Betsy looked at Katy, who seemed to be willing her to stay.

"OK, coffee for three."

Over the next half-hour Betsy looked differently at Allain. Her former anger melted away and she felt as she did the first time he walked into the bistro. Katy was right: he was drop-dead gorgeous.

Chapter Three

Betsy missed Katy. It had been lovely to have company and, what was more, it stopped her thinking too much about Allain. Now she couldn't stop thinking. She was sure he had been sincere – he hadn't intended to embarrass or upset her – and more than that . . . well, was there more than that? She really didn't know. And what about her own feelings? She wasn't sure about those either. And after all, her emotions could not be relied on. She was unhappy and vulnerable. He was just trying to be friendly and apologetic. How could she even begin to think there might be more to it? Plus there was Francesca: he wasn't even available. She was beautiful, successful. What was she thinking? Betsy was shocked at herself – she hadn't even acknowledged her feelings for him until now.

"Stop it," she said forcefully to herself. "You are being ridiculous."

She convinced herself to forget she had ever seen him and to get on with her life. She could never replace Tom, so she shouldn't even try.

It was a quiet week in the bistro; the weather wasn't great and she hoped it would get busier towards the weekend.

As she was helping Julie to set out the tables on the balcony they both noticed a commotion down at the harbour. People were milling about, shouting and then rushing around.

"Oh, look," said Julie excitedly, "they're getting out the lifeboat."

"Oh, Julie, will it be something serious, or could it just be a practice?" questioned Betsy.

"Well, from the sense of urgency and action I think it's a real emergency. Something must have happened out at sea. They're off – look."

"Terrible," replied Betsy.

"Don't worry, Betsy – they are a really great crew. I'm sure they'll rescue whoever is in trouble. It'll probably be a yacht – it usually is."

"But it's calm out there today," responded Betsy. "You'd think it would be stormy weather that would get people into trouble, wouldn't you?"

"You're right," said Julie, "but something has gone wrong out there. We'll have to wait for the boat coming back before we find out."

"Does it happen a lot?" asked Betsy.

"What – the lifeboat going out? Quite often, but it usually has a happy ending. The tides out there are treacherous. A lot of sailors don't realise it and get themselves into trouble. Hey look – Allain Laubert is coming up from the harbour. Perhaps he'll know what's going on."

Betsy hadn't needed Julie to point him out. She had of course spotted him and he was clearly heading for the bistro. She inwardly calmed herself and made the first move to speak. She wanted Allain to know she was clearly prepared to be friends.

"Hello, Allain. We don't normally see you here midweek."

"Hi, Betsy. Yes, I thought to take a couple of days off and get in a bit of extra practice. Have you noticed the lifeboat has gone out?"

"Yes, we've just been watching it. Do you know anything about what's happened?"

"Not really, but Anne in the lifeboat shop was telling me as I walked past that it was a Mayday call from a yacht. Apparently, someone has been taken ill – possibly a heart attack or something."

"How awful! Hope everything works out all right."

"If it's true we'll probably see the helicopter landing soon to take him off to hospital."

"Do you fancy a cup of tea?" asked Betsy.

"That would be nice. Get a cup for yourself – come and join me."

"Are you sure?"

"Sit down – come on, keep me company. It does make you realise how vulnerable you are out there alone on that big wide sea."

Betsy asked Julie to bring the tea, and she joined Allain on the terrace.

"Not very warm out here today," Betsy said. "Are you OK, or do you want to go inside?"

"No, no, I'm fine. This jacket keeps out all the cold."

"I'll just go and get a cardigan, then."

"So, how are you?" he asked when she rejoined him. "Has your friend gone home? She seemed very nice."

"Yes, she had to get back to work. She enjoyed it though, and I loved seeing her. It's been a bit lonely here for me, though I'm feeling more settled now."

"What made you come here, Betsy?"

"Tragedy, depression, misery – I needed to get away, at least for a while."

"I'm sorry – I shouldn't have asked. I didn't mean to pry. It's none of my business, is it?"

"No, it's all right, I didn't think you were prying; and yes, it's a strange place to choose. But my family are from Guernsey originally – at least my grandfather was. Like many others he went over to England to fight in the war and never came back again. He married a Staffordshire woman, my grandma, and stayed there until he died. Yet I know so little about his family or Guernsey, and thought I'd have the perfect opportunity to do a little family research."

"Have you done any?"

"No, not research," Betsy laughed. "I haven't had time, but I did find his house the other day when we met you in Guernsey."

"And what was the real reason for coming here, Betsy?"

"Oh, is it that obvious that I've come to escape?"

Allain smiled and nodded his head. "You don't have to tell me. Perhaps some other time."

"Allain, I'd like to tell you. I haven't told anyone else here. It was my husband, Tom – he died very suddenly about eighteen months ago. I just couldn't cope – couldn't come to terms. Still can't. That was why Katy said I needed to get away. Hence Alderney."

"I'm so sorry, Betsy, and here am I dragging all the grief out of you." And he placed his hand gently over Betsy's and she didn't move it away.

Then a helicopter swept in and landed right on the harbourside. It had obviously done that before.

"Told you it would come, didn't I? The man will be all right now."

Despite the crisis the event served to lighten the mood, the action helping Betsy to recover from her time of woe.

"Anyway, thanks for the tea and company," said Allain, "but I'm off up into town. Thought I might take a look in at the Salon Culinaire while I'm over here. Were you planning to go?"

"No, I have absolutely no idea what Salon Culinaire is."

"Oh, right, well, why don't you walk up with me and I'll tell you all about it on the way?"

"Oh, I don't know," hesitated Betsy. "I can't just wander off when I feel like it."

"'Course you can," insisted Allain. "You put in hours and hours here; you can spare one, surely."

"Well," hesitated Betsy, but she was tempted. "Oh, all right, I'll come. I'm sure Julie can manage. I'll just go and ask her."

They strolled casually up the hilly main street while Allain explained about Salon Culinaire. "It sounds posh, but it's basically Alderney's annual version of a food festival. A couple of chefs come over and cook food, giving free samples; there are food growers and producers too, often from France, mainly Normandy. Then there are cookery competitions for adults and children. A bit like a village fête with people baking cakes, bread, etc."

"It sounds great. I'm really glad you asked me to come."

"Don't get too excited, Betsy," he warned her. "This is the tiny island of Alderney and it's small-scale. But it's still interesting though."

Betsy found it was held in the town hall and was surprised at how busy it was. It was exactly how Allain had described it – small-scale but interesting. They wandered around the rooms, seeing stalls displaying and selling everything from Normandy cider to French cheeses, Alderney cream, venison, French chocolates, wild boar, strawberries and Jersey butter, all locally produced, beautifully presented and with an abundance of free samples. Then they spent some time watching the chefs as they prepared and cooked food expertly. The smells were delicious. In the side room tables were set out for refreshments and Allain suggested they should sit down for a drink and cake. But Betsy wanted to see the competitions first, and was astonished at the number and quality of the entries. After satisfying herself she had seen virtually everything, she acceded to Allain's suggestion of a drink and snack.

"What do you fancy?" asked Allain. "There is some seriously tempting food."

"I know – I can see. And I think I am tempted by a disgustingly gorgeous cream cake."

"Why not? You go and find a table and I'll bring it over. It's my treat."

"Thank you."

Betsy chose a table by a window overlooking a little square and waited for Allain, allowing herself a little time for daydreaming, but not allowing herself to wonder what she was doing here with Allain.

'Just enjoy it, Betsy,' she told herself. 'You are entitled to it. Do you mind, Tom?'

She knew he wouldn't. He would just want her to be happy.

"Here we are," said Allain as he laid everything on the table. "I asked for the low-calorie version, so don't feel at all guilty."

Betsy laughed. "I won't, then. Oh, it looks delicious. Thank you for asking me – I've really enjoyed it."

Then Allain's mobile phone rang.

"I knew I should have switched it off. I suppose I'd better answer it."

"Oh, Francesca, hi there."

He turned away from Betsy, embarrassed, and lowered his voice, but Betsy could still hear his conversation.

"What? Your father? Oh, I'm so sorry. When did it happen? Right. And they took him straight to hospital. Are you there now? It'll be OK. Don't worry – don't get upset. I know, I know. Where am I? I'm on Alderney. I told you I was taking a few days off and decided to sail over. Why? What – you want me to come back? Why, Francesca, there's nothing I can do. I only arrived here a couple of hours ago, I can't sail back so soon. Yes, I know you're upset. OK. OK.

I'll fly back. Yes, I won't delay. I'll come straight away. Calm down. Don't worry – I'll see you soon."

Allain now looked very embarrassed, uncomfortable and unsure what to say or do. His usual unruffled composure had evaporated and Betsy saw a different Allain. He was clearly upset. Betsy looked at him, his green eyes dulled and he turned away.

"I am so sorry, Betsy, but I am going to have to leave you, right now. I have to get back to Guernsey straight away."

"Yes, I heard," whispered Betsy. "You must go – she needs you. What happened?"

"Francesca's father has been rushed to hospital. I'm unsure why – perhaps a heart attack, I don't know. But I'm sure you don't want to hear about it."

He picked up his jacket from the back of the chair and started to walk away.

"What about the yacht?" asked Betsy.

"I'll have to leave her here. It doesn't matter. I'll see you soon. Bye, Betsy."

Betsy didn't reply, she just watched him walk away. She wasn't going to help him feel less embarrassed, or uncomfortable.

The cappuccino and his cream cake were left untouched.

Betsy remained seated at the table. She pushed her cup and plate with the remaining cake away from her. She couldn't face it now – she had suddenly lost her appetite. Once again he had hurt her, upset her, embarrassed her.

'How could he, how could he? I should have known. I've told myself before that Francesca is the important woman in his life. What am I to him? Well, nothing really, that is very clear. He is simply being courteous, kind. How ridiculous am I to think it could be anything else!' Yet she felt the tears trickle down her cheeks, and turned away towards the window so others wouldn't see.

Allain was not in a good temper. 'Damn! Damn you, Francesca! I am not at your beck and call like this, virtually ordering me to come home,' he fumed to himself. Of course he was upset about her father. He had known her parents, David and Susan, virtually all his life, and he sincerely hoped David would be OK. Francesca idolised her father and was truly distraught, but even so. He had been so embarrassed and, if he was honest, very disappointed to leave Betsy. He had let her down again. 'What will she think of me?' Of course he couldn't let Francesca know where he was and whom he was with, but he felt very controlled. It was all getting too much, and he realised he no longer wanted to be with Francesca. This realisation made him almost stop what he was doing with shock. Yet he had to admit that he'd felt like this for a while now, just didn't, couldn't, let the emotion surface in his mind. But with great certainty he now knew it was true. What could he do? Tell Francesca? Yes, but not now when her father was so ill.

What came as an even greater revelation was that it was meeting Betsy that had forced him to acknowledge that he didn't and never had loved Francesca.

'But Betsy – I hardly know her. She's emotionally unstable, she is only here temporarily, and she must now think that I am the last person she wants to see again,' he conceded as he walked out to the plane.

As the plane took off for the short flight he looked down at the sea, Alderney fading into the distance, and the most vivid image in his mind was of a sad-eyed, disappointed, beautiful young woman, pushing away her plate with one hand, and her lustrous auburn hair with the other, an action which didn't quite hide the tears and the hurt in her eyes.

In general Betsy was feeling stronger, and despite the episode with Allain she no longer felt like rushing back to Wrenford on the first plane. This she knew was good. Not that *good* was how she felt – she actually felt humiliated, stupid and very gullible. Yet, despite everything, she knew that Allain had never deliberately hurt her; he had never sought to encourage her to think there could be a future for them. She had known from the start that he had Francesca in his life, that she was a local, like him, and that he had known her family for many years. She only had herself to blame for imagining that he might like her in the same way. She knew better now. 'Don't be so naive!' she chastised herself. 'How old are you? Anyone would think that you were a teenager encountering a first obsession. Yet I have known such wonderful love, I need to hang on to this. Please help me, Tom.'

Nothing though could stop her thinking of Allain. She thought of his assurance, and realised that this was a cover for a greater sensitivity. His beautiful eyes, so full of amusement when she first saw him, became sorrowful, full of guilt and confusion when he had to leave in a hurry.

"Yet we must remain friends," she told herself. "I have a job to do here, responsibilities to my staff. I can't be seen as a quivering idiot whenever I think he may be walking up from the harbour."

In the event if Allain did come back for his yacht, she didn't see him, which did at least mean she didn't have to confront him. Betsy heaved a sigh of relief when after a few days she assumed he must have been and gone. So what did that signify? She just didn't know. On a quiet, sunny day, Betsy strolled down to the harbour. She looked in at the lifeboat shop, introduced herself to Anne, the assistant there, and found out that the man rushed off in the helicopter was OK. Apparently he hadn't had a heart attack at all; he had slipped on deck and broke his kneecap. Painful, but not life-threatening, which was good to hear.

The harbour was quite small and it didn't take long to walk

around and realise that in fact Allain hadn't yet returned to collect the *Jonquil*. Of course he would have had to go back to work, but he must, she knew, be fretting that he had had to leave the *Jonquil* at Alderney longer than he would have liked.

Betsy could see how beautiful a yacht she was – not large, but not small either, she thought. She seemed quite new, white with a picture of a jonquil painted underneath her name. Bobbing gently on the current, she looked like she wanted to go home, Betsy thought, and she knew it wouldn't be long before Allain came to claim her. Betsy continued walking out beyond the sheltered harbour and on to the sea wall. The breeze coming from the sea was fresh but not cold, and she stood and watched as visitors sailed their yachts into the harbour's safety, resting perhaps for a day or a few. No matter, it was, she realised, a beautiful place to stay, and she was surprised how she had come to feel like this. It was a turning point. She no longer felt like a stranger. She was becoming attached to the beautiful small island. Realising too that she was over halfway through the season, she determined on another visit to Guernsey. If she was going to find out anything about her family history, she couldn't wait much longer. She would send her letter to the current occupant of her grandfather's old house and see what happened.

So it was the following Monday on her day off that she found herself on the plane to Guernsey. She was excited and looked back on take-off to see Alderney bathed in brilliant sunshine, the sea beneath a shimmering blue and Guernsey ahead a bulk on the horizon. It wasn't the busiest flight of the day or week – passengers were few and Betsy had found herself up at the front just behind the pilot, and during the short flight he was chatting to her.

"Are you visiting the Channel Islands, then? They are really lovely islands, aren't they?"

"They are," replied Betsy, "but no, I'm not a visitor – well, not quite. I'm actually living on Alderney, though I've only been here a few months."

"And have you settled in?" asked the pilot.

"I have actually. I didn't think I would ever say that – it's taken a while – but I'm really loving it now."

"May not say that in winter though. It can be pretty grim then."

"Yes, I suppose so; but then, so can most places, can't they?"

"That's very true. Anyway, here we go. We're landing on Guernsey now."

Allain had been feeling unsettled. It wasn't like him. He was normally so content with his life and wanted nothing more than he already had. He was surprised. It wasn't a feeling he was used to. He felt frustrated too. Having intended telling Francesca that they needed to cool things down between them, he was annoyed he hadn't had the courage to tell her. She was already upset about her father, but he was on the mend now and Allain realised he would soon have no excuse. Of course Fran wasn't stupid: she had sensed that something was amiss, but was too caught up in her father's welfare to mention anything. What was more, Allain knew he couldn't really blame Francesca for how he felt. It wasn't her fault. In careless moments his mind would slip and the face of another woman would present itself in his mind. Betsy. What was wrong with him? How had this woman got under his skin? Certainly she was different to Francesca. Dark where Fran was fair, brown eyes large and soulful. And with her air of vulnerability she was so opposite to Francesca with her confidence, her family money and her love of clothes and the good life of Guernsey.

But there it was – Betsy had slipped into his life almost without him knowing it, yet he was sure, more than sure, that this wasn't just a passing thing. He realised without a shadow of a doubt that Betsy was important to him. It may have unsettled him and rocked his cosy lifestyle, presenting him with an unaccustomed uncertainty. Yet strangely he wasn't discomfited by this growing awareness. In fact he found himself excited at the prospect, excited at the thought of true happiness on the horizon. 'But hold on,' he told himself, 'how do I know how Betsy feels?' He had every reason to think she must hate him. After all, he had only ever hurt her, embarrassed her and disappointed her. Yet this realisation did not dent his inner belief, not one bit; it only made him even more determined than ever to win her over. He didn't see he had any other choice – his future happiness depended on it. He vowed he would talk to Francesca that evening. He couldn't let it continue. It was wrong. He wasn't the kind of guy who could be with one woman while thinking of another. Allain's whole being was set with determination.

Chapter Four

Allain didn't normally spend his lunchtime in St Peter Port centre, but having been at a meeting he thought he'd spend some time at a bar for a change as it was such a gorgeous day. It was hot, with a cloudless blue sky and tourists were in abundance. Everyone was enjoying the weather, the atmosphere was pleasant and relaxed and he walked to his favourite place down a little cobbled lane, quieter and shady with tables and chairs outside, a perfect venue for a quiet lunch without distractions.

Auberge Victor Hugo was not a magnet for tourists, though in Allain's opinion it should have been; it was unpretentious with good, simple food, local beer and good wine. He sat down at an outside table in the dappled sunshine, the green gingham tablecloths giving it a country feel. The waiter came out almost immediately.

"Allain, we haven't seen you for a while. Are you well?"

"Very well, thank you, Alex. I've been very busy and going back and forth to Alderney. I've entered the yacht race, and think I might have bitten off more than I can chew. How's business?"

"Good," replied Alex. "Yes, very good – can't complain at all. Now, what can I get for you?"

"A pint of my usual, and bring a menu. I'll have some lunch too."

During his brief conversation he hadn't noticed that the person at one of the adjacent tables had turned round to look at him. He was astonished to see Betsy. Neither of them quite knew what to do. Betsy looked as if she was about to get up and leave, but before she could do so Allain jumped out of his seat and went over to her. He didn't allow himself time to think whether or not he should.

"Betsy, no, don't go. Please sit down again – please. I want to speak to you. I can't believe you're sitting here at my favourite little secret haunt."

Betsy hesitated, not knowing whether to stay or go, but without realising she had made a decision she sat down again.

"I don't know," replied Betsy. "I don't know if I want to speak to you."

"Please – I want to apologise. I'm so sorry I left you in the lurch last week. I've been thinking all week about it, wondering what I could do. I shouldn't have just left you, I know that now."

"It's OK, I know how difficult it was for you. How is Francesca's father now?"

Betsy was desperately trying to stay calm, to understand what was going on, making small talk, knowing that deep down she didn't want to walk away from this man. He had hurt her, yes, but she felt there was more to it. She would hear him out and then decide what she would do.

"He's doing OK, but it wasn't a heart attack, you know. It was pneumonia and pleurisy, hence the pain. It's serious, of course, but he's going to be fine. But speaking of Francesca, Betsy, would you mind if I sat down with you here?"

"Yes, OK, just for a minute."

The waiter brought Allain's drink.

"Are you all right for drinks, madam?" asked the waiter.

"Fine, thank you. I still have my coffee. So, Francesca?" Betsy reminded Allain.

He took a deep breath. "One way or another I've known Francesca almost my whole life. We were childhood friends. Our families have known each other for a long time, and Fran's and my parents even holidayed together, and so we were close, and were always friends, but *only* friends. Then somehow it changed." Allain halted, unsure how to continue.

"Go on – it's OK," encouraged Betsy.

"I know I'm just trying to find the right words. I want you to understand," he continued. "Francesca started to be jealous when I had girlfriends and even both sets of parents seemed to think us being together as a couple was simply fulfilling their lifelong expectations. Francesca clearly wanted us to be more than friends. I felt pressured, and it was a pressure I didn't need. I was just building my career, doing well, and didn't want distractions."

"So you agreed to what she wanted."

"Yes – how stupid! It just seemed to solve the problem at the time. But I did explain to Fran that we weren't to get serious, that I didn't want to settle down, didn't see her as my wife. I thought she understood. And for what it's worth we didn't sleep together either, and she didn't like that."

"But she didn't understand?" queried Betsy.

"Oh, I think she understood, just didn't accept it. She simply pretended that everything was fine, that it would be just a matter of time. Then the day at the Salon Culinaire on the telephone, she was so demanding, so domineering. I know she was upset, of course, but it was more than that. It was as if she owned me and would demand anything of me, that I should be at her beck and call. I felt so controlled and trapped. And I realised how I had felt for many months, that I didn't want to be with her, I didn't love her and I would have to do something about it."

"And have you?" Betsy challenged.

"Yes, I told her the truth. It's over between us."

"How did she respond?"

"It doesn't matter, it really doesn't matter."

The waiter had been waiting for an opportunity: "Do you still want the menu, Allain?"

"Oh, sorry, Alex – can you leave it for a few minutes?"

He turned back to Betsy and for a moment a tense silence hung in the air.

Betsy broke the silence: "So why are you telling me all this? It's a very complex apology, and, OK, I accept it."

"It's much more than an apology, Betsy. You see the person sitting right in front of me now isn't the fragile, tragic and vulnerable woman I was led to believe. In fact she's strong, resilient, understanding and very beautiful. And, quite simply, I can't imagine my life without her."

"Allain," Betsy called out, embarrassed, overwhelmed but amazingly happy at the same time.

"What? Have I offended you again? I'm an idiot, blurting it all out like that. What am I like!"

"No, Allain, it's OK," and she reached over, took his hand and beamed at him.

"Is it really?"

Betsy nodded, and smiled again.

"In that case will you let me make it up to you, get to know you better?"

"I'd like that – I'd like it very much."

"Thank you." And he leant over and gave Betsy a tender kiss on the cheek. "Right then, so what are you doing this afternoon? What are you doing over here today anyway?"

"Questions, questions! Well, firstly I came over to finally do some family research."

"Have you managed to discover anything?" Allain asked with interest.

"Do you know, Katy and I managed to find my grandfather's house almost straight away. I never imagined it would even still be here, but I wanted to see it again and I wrote to the address and the woman invited me to see inside; I was on my way after coffee. I can go another time though."

"Where is it, then?"

"In a street called Rue Normandie."

"But that's right in the centre. It must be quite old."

"Oh, it is – it's so quaint."

"That's an old part of town. The houses are all very traditional."

"Yes, it looks like it, but of course I don't know much about it at all. I know it had been a family house for a long time. They were a long-established family here. Of course I'll have to try and find out more."

"What was your family called?"

"Well, I only know of my grandfather and he was Joseph Deauville, but I've got a bit of work to find out anything about the rest of the family."

"Now, we still haven't had lunch. What do you want to do? Have you any plans for the afternoon?"

"No, not really. I can go to the house later, so I've an open afternoon. Why?"

"Because", exclaimed Allain, "I thought I might take you to France!"

"France? You're not serious, are you? How can we go to France? I have to get the evening flight back. You are having me on again, Allain."

"I am and I'm not," he replied mysteriously. "I am taking you to France, but to do it we don't need to leave the island."

Betsy was more confused than ever.

"No, don't ask," Allain said. "I'll explain as we go along. Come on – we'll grab a bite to eat elsewhere."

"But don't you have to get back to work?" protested Betsy as Allain dragged her to her feet and they both set off walking, where to she didn't know.

"No, it's fine – I work for myself, you know. I'll make it up later."

"So are you going to tell me what is going on?" queried Betsy, laughing and enjoying herself.

She had never thought that things would turn out this way. She couldn't quite believe it and she didn't have time to think about what was happening to her. She only knew she felt exhilarated and happy – happier than she could remember for a long time.

"No, I'm not going to tell you yet, but I'll give you a hint. What was the little café where we just were?"

"You mean its name? It was the Auberge Victor Hugo. How is that a clue? You mean Victor Hugo is the clue?"

"Right, and where did he come from?"

"Well, if it's the Hugo I'm thinking of it must be the writer and he was French. So, we are going to France to see where Hugo lived."

"Yes, clever girl."

But Betsy was still very confused. They had been walking, though not very far, and Betsy knew they were in the old part of St Peter Port, with cobbled streets and Georgian houses sloping down towards the town's large harbour.

Allain suddenly stopped in front of a large old house, distinctive and characterful.

"Why have we stopped here?" she asked.

"Because we're here, in France – or we very shortly will be." He laughed as he saw the look on Betsy's face. "OK, I'll tell you now. You see, this is or was Victor Hugo's house."

"Really? So he lived on Guernsey?"

"He did. He came here to live in exile when he was banished from France. He actually finished writing the famous *Les Misérables* here."

"Really? That's amazing!" exclaimed Betsy.

"And he wrote a novel based on Guernsey too, called *The*

Toilers of the Sea, but of course it isn't so well known and didn't become a famous musical," he laughed. "Would you like to go in? It's been kept as it was when he lived here, and it's very quirky and very interesting."

"I would very much like to see it. What a surprise! I never imagined he lived here. I don't suppose many people know it."

"Come on, then."

Allain walked up to the front door and knocked loudly. Betsy giggled as it seemed an odd thing to do. The door was opened by a Frenchwoman whose name badge said 'Mireille', and they were invited in.

"So now you are officially in France," explained Allain. "You see, Hugo's family bequeathed the house to the actual country of France and so it is now officially recognised as part of France. You can see the French flag is flying. That's why you had to knock and be formally admitted."

"Strange," admitted Betsy.

"You see, and you didn't believe me when I said we were going to France. Now do you believe me?"

"I believe you, Allain. Thank you for bringing me. It's so unusual. It's lovely."

After looking round the house they sat in the garden in the sunshine. It was peaceful, serene almost, and yet they were in the centre of the busy town.

"Have you enjoyed it?" asked Allain.

"I have, Allain, so much. It has been so lovely. Thank you!"

"Now, I don't know about you, but I am starving. What do you say to a quick bite to eat and then I can take you up to the airport?"

Later, at the airport, Betsy felt sad to be leaving Allain. It had been a wonderful afternoon, but she wondered if that was all it was. Could she expect more? Would she see him again? Did she want to? All these questions were going round in her head.

As her flight was announced Allain escorted her and seemed unsure what to say.

"Betsy, stop a moment." He took hold of her hand, and looked at her and she could clearly see the tenderness in his eyes. "Thank you for today. I have to come to Alderney and collect my yacht; when I do, would it be OK if I came to see you, perhaps spend a little time together?"

"Yes," replied Betsy, "I would like that very much." She reached up and kissed him on the cheek. "I'll see you then. Give me a call."

She walked on towards the plane, knowing she didn't need to answer any of the questions; she already knew the answer, for Allain had warmed her heart and put a smile on her face. She turned, waved and gave him a big smile. He waved back, smiling in return.

Betsy felt she was in a daze for most of the rest of the week. What had happened seemed almost unreal, yet she knew it was all true. Everything seemed to have turned around. All the misunderstandings had been cleared up. She didn't allow herself to wonder whether what she was doing was wise. She was enjoying her life for the first time since Tom had died. She had a new lift to her spirits and she felt happy to share in the good relaxed atmosphere of Alderney and its beautiful weather. What was more, she felt so much part of it, no longer the outsider. She wasn't going to ponder about any long-term possibilities or the fact that she could get hurt; she was intent on making as much as she could of her time with Allain. Because one thing she was acutely aware of was the fact that in a little over two months' time she would be going home, and what would happen then?

'No, I'm not going to think about it. I'll be like Scarlett O'Hara – I'll think about it tomorrow.' And she put the thought right to the back of her mind.

In the event she didn't have long to wait before she saw Allain again. He came over on the Saturday to sail the *Jonquil* back home. It was a flying visit, but he wanted to spend some time with Betsy before sailing back in the afternoon. He arrived by taxi from the airport and stayed at the bistro only long enough to let Betsy know he had arrived. He then went on down to the harbour to check on his boat. He was relieved to see her still moored in the same place, untouched and looking sturdy and proud.

He looked forward to sailing her home. But he was excited that firstly he had the opportunity to spend some time with Betsy. Of course he too had had all week to contemplate and review what had happened on the Monday. He had no regrets. On the contrary, having spent the afternoon in her company, he had found that his instinct was right: she was everything he had imagined, and he couldn't wait to see her again. Fortunately, too, he hadn't heard from Francesca. She had seemingly accepted what he had said, and that thought too comforted him. He had not wanted to hurt Francesca and hoped they could still be friends, and it was a relief too that she was not confronting him or making it difficult. He hoped that a few weeks avoiding each other might calm the waters, so that eventually they could start off on a new footing. Perhaps, or perhaps he was kidding himself. 'Yes, but what I did was still right,' he stressed to himself. 'If it hadn't been now it would have happened sooner or later. She will have to accept I do not and never did love her.'

Betsy had been watching for Allain as he came up from the harbour, but in the event missed him. When she turned round from behind the bar he was standing looking at her and smiling.

"Hi. How are you today?" he asked her.

"Great. How about you?"

"Never better."

Betsy could see that this was true. It was as if a weight had been lifted from his shoulders. He was relaxed. He was casually dressed in shorts and polo shirt – he looked very much the sailor – and Betsy felt her heart miss a beat, he looked so handsome. For a moment she couldn't quite believe he had come to take her out.

"How was the *Jonquil*? No problems, I hope?"

"No, she's fine, but I'm relieved to see her still here and I'll be glad to get her back to her own berth. What would you like to do? It's a nice day, a bit breezy, maybe even bracing."

"Would you like to just go for a walk?" interrupted Betsy.

"That sounds like a good idea to me."

"We could walk along the coast – perhaps find a sheltered spot on a beach."

"What are you waiting for, then? Lead the way."

They headed down past the harbour and wandered lazily and aimlessly along, and then diverted along a little track, Betsy realising it followed the beach, finally leading to Fort Clonque.

"I've wanted to see this place since I arrived," explained Betsy. "It is such a silly name, but actually it's great, isn't it?"

"It's one of the Napoleonic forts though, isn't it? Not a German one. It's pretty well preserved. You know you can rent it for holidays, don't you?"

"Really? You know everything about this island. I can't surprise you with anything. But what a fabulous place to stay! And you must get cut off – the causeway will get covered at high tide."

"It will. Imagine being marooned out there."

"A bit scary, hey?"

"I don't know – it wouldn't be scary with you, Allain."

Then they both looked at each other, a growing tenderness

almost tangible between them.

Betsy broke the silence. "Well, we're going to have to turn back, seeing we're at a dead end."

"What I haven't seen", announced Allain as they strolled back towards town, "is the Interpretation Centre. It hasn't been open long."

"Where's that, then? Do you want to go?" asked Betsy.

"We could do. I've just noticed the signpost on the road back there. We're not far from it, if you'd like to see it?"

"OK, we might as well. Do you think it will be interesting?"

"I'm sure it will. It's based in one of the original bunkers, you know."

"A German bunker?"

"Yes, there are lots of them here. Many are completely underground, but you can still get into a lot of them."

"There it is, look – near the base of the cliff. Are you sure you want to go?"

"Definitely. It's very much part of Alderney's history, isn't it?"

The bunker was basic, just as it would have been in the war. Built of cold, hard cement, it had been mainly a lookout post over the coastline and the sea. German soldiers were based in it for quite some time and it couldn't have been comfortable. Information boards explained the various elements, and they also gave information about Alderney as a whole. But Betsy couldn't concentrate, for, like Albert said about the campsite, it had a haunted feel.

"I don't like it in here, Allain. It feels cold – an unnatural cold – and there is a very sinister atmosphere. It is holding on to its secrets and they aren't nice ones. It's horrible – I need to get out."

Betsy hurried back to the doorway, wanting to get out into the light and the fresh air. She stumbled as she was going out, crying out as she felt her ankle wrench, and almost fell on to the stony ground. Allain rushed after her.

"Are you all right?"

He helped her to regain her balance and they stepped out into the brilliant sunshine together.

"I'm all right, but I've twisted my ankle a little. I'm sure it'll be fine."

Nevertheless she stood still and leant on Allain's arm until she felt steady.

Then suddenly Allain put his arms around her. Betsy looked up into his concerned face as he bent down to kiss her – a long, sweet, tender kiss, which made Betsy tingle with pleasure.

At the end of the kiss she smiled at him. "Well, you know how to pick your romantic spot, right outside the German World War Two bunker!" And she laughed.

"I know. I'm sorry, but I couldn't resist and I was concerned you had hurt yourself."

"No, it's not too bad, but thank you for being concerned."

And Betsy returned his kiss, melting into his arms, and realised she had been longing for this moment.

"Shall we go and find that beach now?" suggested Betsy when they had both recovered from the realisation of how much they felt for one another.

"I've got a little picnic in my rucksack, and I must say I'm ready for a sit-down and rest."

"I wondered what you had in that bag," Allain remarked as they started the walk down the cliff path to the beach.

It was hot and they took their time and also stopped to listen to the birds – the seabirds shrieking and, nearer to them, a skylark flying up and up singing as it had been disturbed from its nest in the tussocky grass.

"It sounds beautiful, doesn't it, Allain?"

The beach, although it was a weekend, was quiet and secluded. They found a sheltered spot and sat down and relaxed, enjoying the food and wine, the sounds of several oystercatchers and the soft whooshing of the waves on the shore. But they enjoyed each other's company more.

They relaxed in each other's arms, speaking very little, both contemplating what had happened to them but with neither having any regrets whatsoever. Betsy never thought on coming to Alderney to escape her past that she would meet someone like Allain. She was worried she was falling in love and at that moment felt very unsure of her future, hoping it would prove happier than her recent life. 'Please let him love me too,' she thought.

"I'm going to have to go soon, Betsy, if I'm going to get the *Jonquil* back to Guernsey today. And you need to get back to Le Chapeau, I expect."

"I do, but I'd prefer to stay here with you."

Allain brought her face close to him and kissed her again, and then he pulled her to her feet and they set off back to the harbour. Betsy walked down to the yacht with him and felt incredibly sad that he was leaving.

"Listen – if I come over next weekend, would you like to come for a sail on the *Jonquil* with me? I'll sail you round the island and then you will know what I will be encountering during the race."

"OK, Allain, I'd really love that. Thank you, and thank you too for a wonderful day today."

"I enjoyed it too. It has been very special. I'll see you next weekend, then, shall I?"

Then he walked down the jetty and prepared to sail. Betsy started to walk back along the harbour and waved as he stood on the prow watching her. She made her way on to the sea wall and waited for him to sail out and into the open water. He saw her and he waved again, and she watched as he sailed calmly out of sight, the sun glinting on his boat and his sunglasses.

Chapter Five

Betsy felt agitated and impatient all week. Although she tried to calm down, to concentrate on the bistro, it seemed impossible for her to do so. Julie knew what was going on in Betsy's mind; in the few months of working together they had become friends. Also, Betsy phoned Katy, who promised to come over for the weekend of the yacht race. Yet still Betsy couldn't settle. There were nights when she tossed and turned – thoughts, ideas, reservations and uncertainties were going round and round in her head. The weather was hot too. Even with all the windows open her bedroom was uncomfortably hot. She was up very early a couple of mornings, walking along the beach before 6 a.m. The cool dawn air was refreshing, the light had a magical quality and sometimes there was a sea mist and she would sit and watch as it slowly melted and the sun would burn away the rest. Few people were about, but she watched as the few fishermen loaded up with nets and lobster pots and chugged out of the harbour for a long day at sea. Strolling back home she would feel calmer. But why was she so agitated? She asked herself the question frequently, and didn't entirely have an answer for herself. Of course she had no doubts about her feelings for Allain – she knew he was sincere, he cared for her and she sensed this was no fling. But this was the heart of her problem.

'If it isn't a fling and we continue to grow fonder of each other, what then? I'm a mature woman, I've been married, blissfully happy, I know that how Allain makes me feel is the real thing. He makes me happy, he has given me hope for the future. Yet is there a future? How too could I be feeling like this about another man when Tom has only been dead for eighteen months? Oh, Tom, I am so sorry, sweetheart. I feel so guilty. And yet, Tom, my life has to go on. I'm still young; of course I'll never forget what we had. We were so lucky, but is it so wrong for me to want to seek that happiness again? I only know that it doesn't feel wrong. I could easily love this man. What if Allain doesn't love me? Do I just enjoy what we have for now and take the happiness while I can? Can I do that? I don't know. But if he does love me, how can I go home and leave him!'

Betsy knew that worrying wouldn't resolve anything, and towards the end of the week she felt more resigned to let things develop and see what happened. What more could she do? The bistro was very busy too, but, finding a couple of spare hours, she made her way into town for some purposeful shopping. She sought out a couple of the shops aimed at the yachting fraternity, with the intention of buying exactly the right gear for her trip with Allain. She wanted to look the part. She wanted him to be proud of her. Nor did she care how much she spent. It didn't matter. It was enjoyable too chatting to the shop owner as she explained what she wanted and why. In the end she bought everything she could possibly need: deck shoes, espadrilles, a sun hat, shorts, long trousers in case it rained, Breton tops and waterproofs, all topped off with suntan lotion, designer sunglasses and then some seasickness pills just in case.

Just as the rest of the week had been hot, Saturday too dawned bright and sunny. There was no hint of cloud or rain, but Betsy was determined not to abandon the raincoat. She would still take it – no tempting fate.

She was ready and waiting when he arrived at lunchtime, standing on the terrace and waving as soon as she saw him walking up from the harbour.

"Well, don't you look the part?" Allain said when he saw Betsy kitted out in her new expensive yachting gear. "Where did you get everything?"

"Right here in St Anne. They have some lovely things. How do I look? I don't look too 'overdone'?"

"You do not. You look fabulous."

"Thank you."

"So, I assume you're ready. Shall we go?"

"What about lunch?" Betsy questioned.

"All organised – it's all on the boat ready," he answered proudly. "So without more ado shall we go?" And he held out his hand for her.

"Enjoy yourself," called Julie, "and don't go falling overboard."

"I will and I won't," laughed Betsy, and she waved.

They strolled the short way down to the harbour hand in hand.

"Now I know it's very calm out there and we'll have a perfect sail, but, Betsy, please be careful. Keep away from the sides and wear your life jacket at all times."

"I'll be really careful, honestly. I promise."

"Seriously, Betsy, it won't be easy until you get your sea legs." He looked up at Betsy and laughed. "OK, lecture over. Enjoy yourself."

"Oh, she is so lovely," announced Betsy, admiring the *Jonquil*. "How long have you owned her?" And she walked around the little yacht, the two berths, galley and small wheelhouse.

"About three years," Allain replied while preparing to set

sail. "She is beautiful, I know – my pride and joy. Now relax, I'm taking her out."

The engine purred, the sail fluttered in the gentle breeze and Allain eased her to the mouth of the harbour and out to sea, after which he cut the engine. It became quiet and serene. The sun was hot, the breeze warm but refreshing, and the tang of salt and spray assaulted Betsy's senses. It was indeed calm and she stood in the bow and looked back to the island, bathed in sunshine, the last of the gorse lighting up the cliffs, and the seabirds diving all around, emerging from the surf, their mouths stuffed with fish and then returning to their roosts. There were few yachts out, and apart from the birds it was peaceful and exhilarating. Looking ahead, she saw Allain was heading to a small low-lying offshore island.

"Are we aiming for the island?"

"We are. I thought we could have our picnic there. What do you think?"

"What a great idea! Have you been out there before?"

"Been around it, of course, but never landed. There are supposedly lots of puffins here and you can see their burrows."

The island was small and low-lying, probably no more than half a mile long and less than that in width. It was uninhabited except by birds and it was mostly covered in low scrub and gorse, though at one end there were a few trees bent over to one side where they had been blasted by the wind. There appeared to be sandy and pebble beaches all the way around with some sand dunes and rocky, sandy ledges and low cliffs where the birds were roosting and where the puffins probably had their burrows. The island looked deserted and it seemed slightly eerie even in the sunshine. The wailing of the seabirds and the wind buffeting the sails were the only sounds. They passed two large rocks, bare and craggy except for a few little flowers clinging to the edges. Allain told her they were called the Guardian Rocks and they formed the most southerly gannetry in the UK. It was an amazing sight, and the noise was raucous and unabated, the birds themselves large and beautiful. There were thousands of them and Betsy watched them with wonder as they sailed past. Then the smell of the guano assailed them, bitter and pungent, the rocks white with it. The smell was unpleasant and Betsy was glad when there was a greater distance between them and she hoped the smell didn't reach the little island to spoil their picnic.

Then suddenly they had arrived. Her attention having been diverted by the gannets, she hadn't realised the progress they had made.

"We're here, Betsy. Do you want to land?"

"Oh, I do. It's so romantic having a whole island to ourselves. Where will we moor up?" asked Betsy, looking around.

"There are no actual moorings. We'll have to anchor in shallow water and take the dinghy. Can you manage that?"

"'Course I can. Will you have to tack against the breeze? Look at the mainsail – it's really billowing. The breeze is stronger here. But it will be sheltered on the beach. I'll take the lookout for you if you like."

Betsy realised she had given herself away and she looked at Allain, who had an expression of wry amusement and astonishment.

"You are a dark horse. You've done this before. You can sail, can't you?"

"Well, yes, I can, but not very well, and it's some time since I last sailed."

Allain shook his head, once again surprised by Betsy. Allain put the food, blankets and everything else needed for the picnic in the dinghy, and they beached it on the shingly beach and both headed up the beach to find a perfect spot. Blanket, umbrella, windbreak, then food and champagne.

"You are wonderful, Allain. Thank you for going to all this trouble for me."

"It was no trouble, but you aren't going to eat or drink anything until you tell me how you learnt to sail. In fact you've told me hardly anything about yourself and your family. Tell me – I'd like to know more about you."

"Well," began Betsy, "my late husband, Tom, had a yacht and he taught me. We didn't manage to sail her often. She was berthed up in Scotland and it was a long way. But it is so beautiful there, and we both loved it."

"How long were you married?"

"Just six years. Tom was older than me, but he was still only thirty-seven years old when he died. It was tragic."

"What did he do? Did you work too?"

"Not after I married. Tom was a businessman and he also dealt with the stock market. He left me very well off. I don't have to worry about anything financially. But it hasn't made me happy. Life has been awful since his death; I never expected it to change by coming to Alderney, but meeting you, I don't know, it has made me realise that maybe life will not always be sad."

"Oh, Betsy, come here." They both lay down on the beach and Allain took her in his arms and gave her a long, passionate kiss. "You deserve to be happy, Betsy, and if I am helping then I am a happy man."

Then Allain brought out the food – smoked salmon, crab sandwiches, salad and cold Jersey potatoes washed down with champagne, followed by strawberries and raspberries with cream.

"That looks delicious," confessed Betsy. "You're an expert picnic maker. And this whole day is perfect. I can't remember when I last felt so relaxed, peaceful and happy."

"I'm really enjoying it too," agreed Allain. "But we haven't got very far in terms of sailing around the island, have we? What do you want to do?"

"I would really like to stay here for a while. It's so beautiful. But then what do you say to sailing just around this little island, and looking for those puffins you mentioned? I haven't seen any yet."

They packed up the picnic basket, but continued drinking the champagne. Then they relaxed in each other's arms, dreamy, relaxed, Betsy a little light-headed, and not just because of the champagne.

Before returning to the *Jonquil* they decided to walk around the island and see if they really could see puffins. There were no footpaths, but tracks had been beaten down by many footprints all heading to the same spots. They followed a well-trodden path around the edge of the beach, where it turned inland and where the island rose towards the small rocky outcrop.

Allain took Betsy's hand to help her up and they soon saw the little burrows dug into the side of the crag where the rock was soft and shaly. Allain put his fingers to his lips; he knew that if they were to have any chance of seeing a puffin they would need to be deathly quiet. So, finding some tussocky grass and sandhills, they both crouched and waited. Betsy didn't care how long they would need to wait, or indeed if they would see them at all. Yet almost immediately they both saw a squat little bird fly in and land just outside a burrow. Its bulbous colourful beak was packed with little sand eels. It looked around furtively, but assured of its safety it disappeared into the burrow. Allain and Betsy slithered down the crag and then sat down at the edge of the beach. Allain looked at Betsy, her eyes alight and with a grin from ear to ear.

"I take it you were pleased at seeing that?"

"It was amazing. They do look so funny, don't they? But so endearing! I feel so lucky – I've never seen one before. The sea and everything is so much part of your life, Allain; but for me, I would have to travel a couple of hours to the sea from where I live in Warwickshire."

"To be honest, I don't see them very often. There may be wildlife all around, but you don't often see it."

Then they were back on the yacht and sailing home, but ensuring they circumnavigated the tiny island first, wondering if they would see the same or a different little puffin on the way. They were unlucky this time, but it didn't matter; there would, she knew, be other times.

Although Betsy felt a bit of a novice compared to Allain, she found all the sailing skills coming back to her as they sailed for home. She helped him with the ropes, attending to the sails and all the time feeling the splashes of salty sea and enjoying the sun and breeze.

"A good job I remembered the suntan lotion," she said. "I'd forgotten how much I enjoyed this. Tom used to love it so, and it is so invigorating – the feeling of freedom and mastery of the sea. It's a pity we couldn't stay longer with the puffins, but there is always another day."

As they turned back for Alderney the wind freshened and changed direction. The mainsail billowed and rattled; Betsy's hair became tousled and wild. They both put on a jumper and felt glad they were heading back. A few clouds scudded across the sky, and it was becoming overcast as they sailed safely into harbour.

As Allain helped her on to the quayside, Betsy felt a bit wobbly and laughed. "I don't know whether I'm still a bit tipsy or whether I haven't yet got my proper sea legs."

"Probably a bit of both. But really, Betsy, you have been brilliant. You'll be competing against me in next year's Challenge at this rate."

"I don't think so. I don't think I'll even be here. I go home in September, you know."

"Let's not think about that," said Allain, and they were both subdued as they walked back to the bistro, but also elated, windswept and tired.

Betsy had to prepare herself for a busy night's work, and she knew it would be difficult. She couldn't get her mind into gear. She was tired and she couldn't forget the idyllic time she had spent with Allain. After coffee together, Allain prepared to leave, knowing she had a busy evening ahead.

"Are you going to be all right?"

"Of course. I've taken on extra staff for the weekends, so I'll be fine."

They walked outside to the terrace, where it felt chilly, and he wrapped her in his arms.

"I don't think many people will want to stay out here for long this evening."

Betsy pulled herself slightly away from him. "Allain, do you want to stay tonight?"

"There is nothing I would like more, but you will only be finishing work in the early hours and you're already tired. You'll be absolutely shattered. Another day though, and soon, because I just can't wait."

He drew her back to him and kissed her passionately, with longing and, more importantly, with love. He pulled away from her.

"I'll stay on the boat tonight, grab a snack at the yacht club. Now you go – you need to get ready."

She watched him go, waving until he was completely out of sight.

Physically, Betsy was well prepared for her busy night; mentally and emotionally she was far away. She found herself continually remembering her wonderfully day, and concentrating on the here and now was demanding more from her than she felt able to give. In a few quiet moments she was able to confide in Julie the events of her day and how she felt about Allain. Julie hugged her and said how delighted she was.

"Go for it, Betsy. Go for it while you can. He's gorgeous and genuine."

"I think so too," agreed Betsy, and they both grinned.

For the first time since taking the job, Betsy was relieved when she was finally able to lock up at the end of a long, busy but memorably wonderful day. She barely remembered getting into bed, where she immediately fell into an exhausted sleep, tempered by very sweet dreams.

For Allain, however, sleep was a long time coming. The wind had dropped, the night was still and peaceful, and the gentle bobbing of the boat and the lapping of the sea against the pontoon would normally speak to him of comfort, freedom and pleasure and would lull him into a deep untroubled sleep. This night was different. He had never experienced these feelings before and hadn't been prepared for them. He knew without a doubt that he had fallen in love with Betsy, yet he was confounded by it. He had always enjoyed his single life, never really considering the idea of settling down and certainly never expecting to fall in love. If and when he did he'd always believed it would be someone from Guernsey, a woman familiar with island life. When he was at university on the mainland he never entertained the notion of settling there, and always returned home knowing he would want to remain in Guernsey all his life if he could. Now here he was not only falling in love, but even seriously considering the possibility of marrying a woman from Warwickshire, who was due to return there in a month's time.

What if she didn't love him? What if she didn't want to marry again? What if she preferred to live in England? He felt agitated at the thought that he might lose Betsy, and became disconcerted and even slightly panicky at the thought that she had turned his life upside down. He couldn't imagine his life without her. And what was it about her that had stolen his heart? Certainly she wasn't like most of the women he knew and had dated on many occasions. They were mostly professional women, from wealthy families, privileged and comfortable, stylish but class-conscious. Had he realised that maybe this wasn't the kind of woman he wanted? A picture of Betsy came into his mind, and he knew it was a picture of what he saw as a perfect woman. She was unassuming, but intelligent, kind, appreciative. She was brave and resilient, not angry or bitter at what life had dealt her. And he saw too that she was beautiful, not in a done-up sophisticated way but a natural beauty – a beauty which was enhanced from within by an inner sparkle, sincerity and serenity.

Whatever had happened to Allain, however unexpected, he had no regrets. Indeed it was, he realised, the exact opposite. He could not think of a better alternative future for himself other than to be with Betsy. And in that moment of true realisation he fell asleep and was untroubled, happy and optimistic.

In the early morning Betsy walked down to the harbour to greet Allain, and they shared coffee and then Allain made toast.

"It's only two weeks to the Challenge now, Betsy. I've got a really busy week at work next week, so I think I'm going to have to head home this morning. I want to do a bit of work and maintenance on the *Jonquil*, and I won't have time after today."

"Must you go?"

"I don't want to, but I feel I must if I'm going to be properly prepared. Plus I promised Mum and Dad I'd have dinner with them today. It's my brother James's birthday this week and they want a little family get-together. I'm sorry, Betsy, but maybe we can get together in the week. Do you suppose you could fly over?"

"I'll try, but the bistro is busy too. I'll see if Julie will take over for a day."

"Try, then. I'd love to see you." He gave her a hug and kiss. "Now I must go, Betsy. Take care and I'll see you in the week."

Betsy stepped off the yacht as Allain prepared to sail. He was soon gone and Betsy felt somehow forlorn, her eyes moist, but she felt a contentment deep inside. After returning briefly to the bistro, she changed and went to church. She felt calm and uplifted as she prayed and shared all her feelings, concerns and emotions with God. She returned refreshed, ready for the day ahead in time to open up for lunch. There were families on the beach below, playing cricket, making sandcastles. She shared their pleasure, sensing an optimism she hadn't felt for a very long time.

'Thank you, Allain. You have given me hope, a purpose, a longing to move forward with my life.'

So, with a spring in her step, she worked enthusiastically, sharing conversation and jokes with locals and visitors alike. No one could have known that only six months ago she was still a grieving widow, facing what she had thought was a long, bleak future. Over recent weeks that future had blown away like the early morning mist, to be replaced by a bright optimism.

Chapter Six

"No, Katy, you and Patrick can stay here."

"But you only have the one bedroom. Where will you sleep?" Katy replied sternly.

"Look – it's the big event of the year here. It brings in hundreds of visitors. There aren't many hotel beds in Alderney to start with, and I have no doubt that they will all be booked now. Probably been booked for months. Honestly it will be fine – I can sleep on the sofa bed in the living room. It won't be a problem."

"Betsy, are you really sure?"

"For goodness' sake, Katy, I'm sure. It will be just wonderful to see you both. But listen – you must book your flight very soon. The planes get booked up too – not everyone comes by yacht."

"Will do," replied Katy confidently. "I can't wait to see you. Patrick is looking forward to it too – it will be a lovely break for us both. He is so tired and it still seems such a long time away from our holiday in October. How's the weather, by the way? Is it still hot? Will I need suntan lotion and glasses?"

"It's glorious, Katy; and yes, you will need both."

Katy asked, "Is Allain all prepared, then?"

"More or less. He's spending what time he can this week

doing some maintenance work and any improvements he can think of. He's getting quite nervous."

"I'm not surprised – it's so exciting. I've never been to a yacht race before. I can't wait. And, Betsy, I can't believe all you've told me about him. I'm so pleased for you. He seems so kind and caring – wonderful really, lucky thing."

"I know, Katy, but there is no certainty about it. I've only about five weeks left here, and what will happen then is anyone's guess."

"You don't want it to end though, do you? You've got to try and make it work."

"I know and I will," Betsy said to her friend, but there is nothing certain, is there? He won't leave Guernsey – he loves it too much."

"Don't sound so defeatist, Betsy. Love will find a way, as the saying goes."

"Yes, well, maybe. Anyway, I'll speak to you soon, and see you soon too. Take care, Katy. You are my precious friend – love you."

"You take care too, sweetie – love you."

Betsy put down the telephone. It had been great to speak to Katy. She didn't feel so lonely in Alderney now, but it was still nice to have someone who was there for her.

It was Betsy's day off and she felt exhausted. She had slept in late, had a long leisurely breakfast and had no plans at all for the rest of the day. She wasn't sure she was even going to make any plans, other than relax, sit on the balcony, watch the world go by and perhaps read her book. A relaxing day would do her good. If she felt like it, later she could walk up into town, do a little shopping and perhaps buy something new for when she met Allain later in the week. She even knew a few people now and might meet someone on the walk through town, spend a few minutes in idle conversation and then find a coffee shop, sit outside and daydream.

In retrospect the relaxing day had been a very good idea, because Tuesday proved to be a fraught day, troublesome and upsetting. Betsy had experienced few such days in her time at the bistro, but this would be one day she would probably never forget.

Tuesdays weren't normally the busiest of days, and it was a good time for Betsy and her staff to sort out any problems, do some extra cleaning, plan the specials for the week and catch up on any news. This looked like being a typical Tuesday. There were a few morning customers for coffee and cakes, tea and scones, but lunchtime customers seemed likely to be few and far between.

Both Betsy and Julie made the most of the quiet time, sitting outside with a long, cool drink.

"Well, Julie, customers or no, I suppose we'd better get on, hadn't we? Could you make up the specials board?"

"'Course – I'll get on to it now."

"Thanks," replied Betsy. "Oh and look – here comes Henry. That means we really must make a move. Come on, Jules."

And they both moved indoors.

The specials had proved popular over the season, especially the seafood, for which Alderney was respected. But the simplicity and ambience of the bistro had proved equally popular, the scrubbed pine tables and floors, and fresh flowers on a daily basis – a job Betsy always liked to do, often walking and picking wild flowers, which grew in profusion. They gave the bistro a rustic, homely feel, but at the same time it was chic and elegant. Betsy had come to love it and she knew she had done much to improve both its look and its atmosphere.

Betsy felt relaxed. The few customers were sitting on the terrace, the inside virtually empty. Julie was pottering, Henry singing to himself as he prepared for the lunchtime customers.

"You sound happy today, Henry. We all seem quite content, don't we? How lovely."

Henry popped his head out of the kitchen, and leant against the door. Betsy turned as he replied, "It's a lovely day, a beautiful place, and the promise of some gorgeous food coming up. Yes, I suppose you could say I'm happy today. You look bright and cheerful yourself, Betsy. Being in Alderney has done you good."

"You're right, Henry, it has, and having you and Julie has helped. You have made me feel so welcome, and we've run this place as a brilliant team."

"Oh, customer, Betsy – I'll get back to my kitchen."

Betsy turned to greet the customer and froze. Her stomach lurched and she felt nauseous, but she tried not to show it. The customer was Francesca. What should she do? What could she do? She wouldn't ignore her – she wasn't that kind of person – nor would she ask Julie to take over. Although Julie had sensed Betsy's reaction, she continued sorting out the cutlery while keeping an eye on the drama unfolding in front of her. She knew Francesca, of course, well before Betsy did – she had often accompanied Allain in the previous season – and she didn't like her. She had found her snobbish and conceited. Her family clearly had money and she appeared spoilt. Her clothes were expensive. She was certainly a head-turner and yet, in her favour, Julie conceded, she wasn't a flirt. She seemed devoted to Allain, and therein, she knew, lay the crux of the drama.

'What is she doing here?' Betsy asked herself. 'She's alone and must have flown over this morning.' But why? She didn't have business here – or at least not that Betsy knew. And why come to Le Chapeau? There were other eateries. It pointed only one way: had she come to confront Betsy? 'Please, no, don't let it be that, and not here. Whatever happens, I must be civil, polite and accommodating.'

"Are you serving lunch yet?" She addressed Betsy.

"Certainly. We can take your order whenever you wish."

"OK, I'll look at your specials, then." And she walked over to the board.

Betsy could see she had made a particular effort with her appearance. She was casual, wearing jeans and a long linen tunic, with a long heavy necklace and earrings. Her make-up was immaculate, her strawberry-blonde hair shiny and healthy and gliding across her shoulders. Casual she may have been, but she looked stunning and she knew it. Betsy, on the other hand, though tanned and glowing, was wearing the barest of make-up, black trousers and flat comfy shoes, and she was several inches shorter than Francesca.

Francesca strolled casually back to the counter to where Betsy stood, and Julie too now.

"I see you have lobster and crab."

"Yes, totally fresh, brought in early this morning. We don't always manage to get it, but when we can it's delicious. Henry is a wonderful chef." Betsy knew she was rambling, desperately trying to cope.

"Oh really?" answered Francesca in a very stuck-up way. "I don't suppose you could ever afford to eat lobster before you came here, could you? So expensive and sophisticated."

"Well, actually yes, I did, many times," answered Betsy calmly.

"A likely story. I mean, how did you manage it? An ordinary bar person like you!"

Betsy: "Manage what? I don't know what you mean."

"Oh, come on – you set your mind on him, didn't you? He must have been drunk – I can't think of any other reason why he would be remotely interested in you. I mean, look at you. But I suppose he can't see you when the lights are out."

There was an audible gasp from Julie at this woman's audacity, but Francesca continued, oblivious and unabashed.

"You think you've made a good catch, eh? Well, let me tell you, you have no chance. I mean, look at us. Whom do you think he will choose when he comes to his senses? Not poor little Miss Ordinary with no prospects. Anyway, I'll have the crab sandwiches."

And she went and sat down.

Betsy was pale and shaking and Julie was almost shaking with rage.

"You can't let her speak to you like that," a shocked Julie said.

"No, it's OK, Julie, leave it. I'm not lowering myself to her level."

"But what she said was so unfair, untrue. She's horrible."

"Yes, you're right, but she also feels slighted and can't believe what Allain has done to her. I'm not going to make it worse for her."

"You are too soft for your own good."

"Maybe, but I'd rather be like me than like her."

In the meantime, Henry had also appeared.

"I heard shouting. Is everything OK here?"

"Yes, it's all right, Henry, really, but thanks for your concern."

"Well, don't forget I'm here if you need me."

He looked straight at Francesca in an intimidating way. Francesca ignored him.

"I'll have a large white wine too. I don't suppose you have Chablis?"

"Not by the glass; only by the bottle."

"Oh, I can afford a bottle. I'll have that."

"Right. I'll see to it, Betsy," insisted Julie.

The atmosphere was awful. Betsy was only glad no other customers had come in. Everyone felt on edge, but, with a whole bottle of Chablis to drink, Francesca wasn't for moving on for a while yet.

'And when she's drunk, how will she behave then? Oh, Francesca, just go – please go.'

But go she didn't and, unlike the staff, she appeared relaxed and unperturbed. There was no knowing if she really did feel like that – maybe she was a good actor. Henry brought the crab sandwiches and Betsy took them from him, intending to serve Francesca herself.

"Let me do it." And Julie moved to take them from her.

"No, I'm not going to let her think she has the better of me. I'll go. I'll be fine. Here you are, Francesca, your crab sandwiches. Hope you enjoy them."

Francesca looked down her nose at Betsy with disdain.

'Keep calm and carry on,' Betsy told herself.

"How is your father? I hope he is recovering well."

"Oh, please, don't pretend you care about my father. And anyway, why should I want to discuss him with you?"

"Sorry," replied Betsy very quietly. "I meant it sincerely."

"Well, thank you. As it happens he is making a fine recovery. But then, you see, we can afford the best care and treatment for him. We are all determined that only the best will do for Daddy!" Francesca's voice was getting louder by the minute. "I suppose if you had had some money you could have had better care for your husband, and maybe he wouldn't have died."

Betsy's eyes filled with tears. Any sympathy she had felt for Francesca evaporated. Cruel – how could she be so horribly cruel?

Betsy turned to walk away, but not before Francesca saw she had really got to her this time. Realising she had brought her to tears, a triumphant smirk spread across her face. At the same time Betsy saw Henry and Julie start in anger heading for Francesca's table. Betsy put up her hand and shook her head, insisting they did not approach her.

"Bitch!" exclaimed Julie. "Come on, Betsy – come

and sit outside. The company is far too sordid in here," making sure Francesca heard her.

Henry disappeared back into the kitchen, slamming the door behind him.

Francesca simply smirked and continued to drink her wine.

Outside both Julie and Betsy walked down to the seat on the path leading to the beach.

"Before you ask, yes, I'm OK."

"You are far from OK, and I am not surprised."

"She isn't worth discussing, is she? But I do feel a bit shaken. Would you go and get me a strong coffee and put a large dash of whisky in it?"

"I certainly will. It will do you good. And no coming back until she's gone. I mean it."

"All right, I don't want to anyway. I don't ever want to see that woman again."

Julie left her to go back to the bistro, and, now alone, Betsy let her tears fall. Tears of anger, sadness, confusion and frustration.

'What have I done? I never should have come here. I'm just not ready for all this. I don't need another relationship – what I had with Tom was enough for a lifetime of love. Should I go home and let Allain and her sort it out between them? Perhaps it would be for the best. I never meant this to happen. I'm just as bad as she is.'

Yet, despite everything, Betsy still had a desperate longing for Allain. She knew she loved him.

'But if it would end all of this, I'll give him up. I'll go home and try to put it all behind me.'

Julie arrived with the coffee.

"Thank you, and thank you for being so understanding. I don't think I could have coped in there completely on my own."

Julie didn't say anything. She just patted Betsy on the shoulder and dashed back. Betsy knew she was lucky to have Julie, both as a waitress and as a friend. She was a lovely, kind unassuming person. Born and living all her life on Alderney, she had been married to Joe for over twenty years, had two grown-up children and was totally happy and content with her life. She told Betsy she had no inclination to live anywhere else. Yet despite being part of the close community of Alderney she had found time to be friends with her, and they had come to care for one another.

Julie felt the same way and she was determined not to let Francesca get away with her atrocious behaviour. She knew Betsy had said not to get involved, but she need never know, and she wasn't there. It was time for Francesca to hear a few home truths.

"I hope you are proud of yourself," she launched at Francesca as soon as she walked in. "How could you? Yes, you may be upset about Allain, but that doesn't entitle you to be cruel and contemptuous. And no, don't think you can leave now!" – as Francesca got up to go. "There are a few facts you might be interested in."

Reluctantly Francesca sat down.

"Firstly, Betsy is most definitely not 'just', as you put it, a poor ordinary barmaid with no prospects, and with an eye for a good catch. She doesn't need to be a gold-digger – she has enough money of her own."

"A little payout from her husband's life assurance doesn't count as being wealthy, you know," Francesca scoffed.

"Look, you snob – Betsy is not just Betsy Abbot; she is Lady Rowanden. Her husband, Tom, was an aristocrat and, thanks to his business acumen, he was also incredibly wealthy and so is she. Not everyone is like you – she doesn't flaunt her wealth or advertise her background. She didn't *need* this job. The reason she came here is her affair, but it wasn't because she needed employment. She could buy out you and your family if she so wished, and your house will probably fit into hers ten times over!"

All this time Francesca became more and more quiet, stunned and shocked.

"I don't have to take this from you," she bellowed at last.

"Well, I haven't quite finished yet. Your comment about her husband – how dare you say that to anyone! Do you have no compassion? Tom died at thirty-seven, for goodness' sake. He was dead before he even got to hospital. No amount of money could have saved him. Now get out – we don't want you here. Take your Chablis and go. And don't think Betsy put me up to this. She didn't."

Now totally speechless, Francesca got up from the table, left a pile of notes and the rest of the wine and hurriedly left. Julie herself was shocked and overcome by what had happened, but she was glad she had spoken to Francesca all the same.

"Good grief, Jules," laughed Henry, who had overheard everything, "that was some speech. You were marvellous. That's taken her down a peg or two."

"Yes, but that isn't why I said it. I just couldn't let her get away with all those hurtful things she said. Plus, I wanted her to know the truth. Bloody snob!"

And they both laughed, mostly with relief.

"What are you two laughing at?" asked Betsy, who had just returned.

"Nothing – we're just glad she has gone."

"Mm, I saw her heading up to the yacht club, so thought it was safe to come back. Seeing it's so quiet, do you suppose I could take a few hours off?"

Two days later Betsy was still upset by the encounter, but she was determined to meet Allain in Guernsey and say nothing about what had happened. In reality though, she knew it would be hard. She worked over lunch and then, when Julie came to take over in the afternoon, Betsy left to catch a late flight to Guernsey. It would be a short visit – she needed to work the next day. Allain met her at the airport, holding out his arms to give her a big hug.

"Flight OK?"

"Fine, yes. You know, I feel just like a local now, flying back and forth on those little planes. I'm quite used to them now. Do you have to go back to work?"

"No, no, it's fine. I can always catch up at home."

"Are you sure?" Betsy questioned. She didn't want to cause him problems with work. "I can always entertain myself – do a bit of people-watching. It looks like it's going to be a lovely evening. I really wouldn't mind."

"Betsy, it's fine. Watch my lips: it is fine." And then, just when she wasn't expecting it, he bent and gave her a tender kiss.

Betsy giggled. "Well, OK, so what is the plan? Do we have one?"

"We certainly do. We'll go back to my place, and I'm going to cook you dinner. Then we can sit out on my balcony with a glass of wine and watch the world go by. How does that sound?"

"It sounds fabulous. And after dinner?" Betsy blushed.

"Well, now that depends, doesn't it?"

"Does it? On what?"

"On you, Betsy."

"Oh."

And she was quiet, slightly embarrassed and also aware that this could be a very important decision for her. She knew precisely what she wanted to do, and yet at the same time she was desperately afraid. They reached Allain's car and she was glad of the momentary distraction of getting in and driving off to hide her unease. Of course she knew Allain had his own apartment in St Peter Port, but didn't know quite what to expect. In fact it turned out to be the penthouse in a tall twenty-first-century block of flats, all glass and steel and full of light. Allain's penthouse was large and tasteful, though the decor was that of a single man, but the outlook was awe-inspiring, with huge full-length windows looking out right over the harbour, the sea and castle and the islands of Herm and Jethou. Without a shadow of a doubt Betsy knew it must have cost a fortune. It was one of the most enviable situations in town.

"Oh, Allain, it's gorgeous, and you don't need to tell me why you chose this view. You can wave to the *Jonquil* every morning when you look out."

"Exactly, and of course the *Jonquil* can smile back at me too."

They both laughed and immediately felt totally at ease.

"How long have you lived here?" Betsy asked.

"Not long actually – just over a year – but I knew I wanted this place even before it was built. I bought off-plan, and of course because I was buying the penthouse it was the last bit to be built. Worth the wait though, don't you think?"

"Definitely – it's really gorgeous."

"There's more yet – come on, I'll show you."

And he took Betsy through the kitchen, out and up a couple of steps on to a roof garden. There was a green roof, looking exactly like a lawn, with a table and chairs and a small swimming pool. It was sheltered by an enclosing wall.

"Wow!" Betsy was lost for words. "I've never seen anything like it. A bit misleading to call it a balcony." And she laughed.

"Fancy sitting and sampling a nice glass of wine?"

"Definitely," answered Betsy, full of awe.

Nor did Allain go back inside to get it, but he took a bottle from a small fridge by the side of the pool.

"Sit down and enjoy the wine," Allain said, pouring her a large glass. "There is something I've got for you. I'll just get it." He returned with a parcel wrapped in beautiful paper and tied with a ribbon. "This is for you, Betsy. I thought you'd like it. It's very evocative of the Channel Islands."

"Oh, Allain, thank you." And she started to open it. "A jumper! Oh, it's lovely, thank you."

"No, not just a jumper, you idiot – it's a guernsey."

"Right, but it's pink. I thought all guernseys were blue or brown."

"Not any more. They come in all sorts of colours – still warm and waterproof though. I thought you would look great in it when we go out on the yacht again."

Betsy was very touched, and with the effect of the wine too she unwittingly lapsed into memories of Francesca's visit, the uncertainty of everything and the thought that her stay on Alderney would soon be up. Once again she felt sad, and unsure what she wanted. Allain noticed she had become quiet, almost subdued. He pulled his chair closer and took her hand.

"What is it? Have I done something, said something, to upset you?"

"No, no, you could never do that." And she reached up and stroked his cheek.

"What, then? Something is wrong."

"I told myself I wasn't going to say anything – I didn't want to spoil our precious time together – but I can't stop thinking about it."

"Thinking about what? You must tell me."

Betsy shook her head, but Allain looked at her in such a way that she knew he was determined to hear about it.

"It was on Tuesday – Tuesday lunchtime – in the bistro. Francesca came in. It was so awful, Allain. She said some terrible things. She loves you and hates me – blames me for taking you from her. I don't need all this, Allain. I came to Alderney to find some inner peace. Perhaps we would be better not being together. I go home in a few weeks – maybe it's for the best. Perhaps you and Francesca can sort things out when I'm no longer here." and Betsy sobbed.

Allain had become very quiet. She could sense he was seething underneath what appeared a calm exterior.

"Francesca – you mean she came over to Alderney specially to see you?"

"Yes, I think she did. Julie and Henry were great, but it was so embarrassing."

Allain wasn't going to say any more about Francesca, but he was incandescent. 'How dare she! Who does she think she is? Has she not got the message yet?' He went to Betsy and put his arms around her in a tight hug.

"I am so sorry, but you must listen to me: Francesca has no claim on me. I do not love her, never have and have no intention of ever even considering having a relationship with her. You going back to England will not make a scrap of difference. Watch my lips and listen: I love you, no one else, not now, not ever. Do you believe me, Betsy? You must, because it is true. I never considered I could fall in love, or so deeply, but I love you until it comes out of my ears. And please don't talk about going back to England – I can't bear to think about it."

Betsy's eyes glistened with tears. She wiped them away, smudging her make-up. She smiled through her tears.

"I love you too, Allain. I didn't expect to fall in love either, but I couldn't help myself. I think I fell in love that very first time you walked into the bistro. But I'm afraid too, Allain. It has all happened so quickly and us finding happiness has hurt other people."

"It doesn't matter," emphasised Allain. "Don't be afraid. It will all be wonderful, honestly. I promise. I love you, Betsy. Let me prove it."

Suddenly they were both consumed by passion. Both stood up. They looked longingly into each others eyes.

"Come on," Allain whispered.

He took her hand, led her inside. Betsy had no doubts as to where he was leading her and she knew she would follow him willingly into his bedroom and into his bed. No longer was she afraid. She wanted him; she knew she could trust him. She tingled as he touched her, falling together on the bed, and despite their urgency Allain took time to explore her body, drinking in her perfume, her anticipation, until finally they could not wait any longer. She sighed with deep longing and then with deep pleasure as they made love and they both knew that they had become deeply and madly in love.

Later, after lying contentedly in each other's arms, Allain slid off the bed.

"I've realised we never got around to having dinner. Do you fancy something to eat now?"

"Definitely," Betsy answered him with a huge grin. "I feel like I could eat a horse."

Chapter Seven

Allain was in something of a quandary. He was furious with Francesca for many reasons – not least the way she had spoken to Betsy and the fact she had deliberately gone to Alderney to exact her revenge. How could she think such actions could result in her favour? All it had done was to reinforce what she was really like, which clearly highlighted her arrogance, her ignorance and her vengeful nature. Not that he cared any more; if anything he was glad that he could now clearly see what she was like. But she had really gone too far. His uncertainty though centred around what he should do about it. Knowing Francesca as he did, he knew that if he confronted her about what had happened she would react smugly, realising she had got his attention, and this of course is what she wanted. Yet not doing anything about her appalling behaviour was also an unclear path to take. She would then think that he obviously didn't care that she had insulted Betsy, and would hold up her hopes that he did still love her after all. Either way he knew he couldn't win and so he determined to take the easy way out and not contact her at all. At the end of the day he realised that it didn't matter what she thought. Her feelings were irrelevant, but hopefully she might realise her play had backfired. He had more important things to contemplate without worrying about what Francesca thought about everything. Betsy was the injured party and Allain had no doubt at all where his attention and his loyalty should lie, and where he should focus his love and support. He had never before felt such deep feelings of love, mesmerised as he was by what was happening to him. Nothing and no one, including Francesca, would divert him and spoil this new and special feeling he was experiencing.

Allain also knew he needed to come back down to earth. He had to work, and he had to make his final preparations for the yacht race, now less than ten days away. He had only one final weekend to finalise his plans and put all his careful preparations in place. He knew though that there was little else he could do. If he wasn't ready now, he never would be.

'I need to take some time out to relax, but I know I'll be so nervous on the day.'

The long-range weather forecast was predicting some changeable weather.

'That's all right, as long as it isn't too windy. I can plan accordingly,' he convinced himself. 'What's more, I'll have Betsy there, coaxing me, encouraging me. I couldn't ask for more.'

On Alderney Betsy was also thinking about the race, but in a more mundane fashion. She and her staff were planning for the big weekend. Julie had already explained that it would be like nothing she had experienced so far.

"So will I really need to take on even more staff, Julie?"

"Definitely. The crowds and the resulting extra trade will be phenomenal. Of course the location of the bistro near the harbour too means we will get the early fall-out – people heading here before going up into town."

"Oh dear! Will we cope, do you think?"

"'Course we will. Don't worry about it. The main thing will be to enjoy it all. Of course we'll be really busy, but not overwhelmed, and the atmosphere is really fantastic. People just want to enjoy themselves. There'll be very little trouble, despite the mayhem. Everyone is really well behaved."

"What about you, Henry? Are you happy you'll have enough help in the kitchen?"

"Yes, yes. The main worry for me is getting enough food supply, especially the seafood, but I'll cross a few palms to make sure it gets delivered here before anywhere else." And he laughed.

"I'll leave that to you, then," smiled Betsy in return.

"The other thing", continued Henry, "is it may take a bit longer for customers to get their orders, but I think people will be in such a good mood they won't really mind."

"Well, let's hope not. We don't want them moving on elsewhere."

"We'll make sure they don't."

"One last thing," added Julie: "we need to get in some extra stocks of certain drinks – champagne, Pimm's, G & T. One thing we can't run out of is people's favourite tipples. Shall I arrange that?"

"That would be great, Julie. Is there anything else?"

Silence prevailed.

"Right, then, meeting over. We all know what we need to do between now and the race, so let's get to it. And it's opening time now too."

Betsy was finding that she had boundless energy and enthusiasm. Nothing seemingly worried her and she was excited and could hardly wait until race day. The only thing to mar her mood was that she and Allain would not have much time together – almost none, in fact. They were both so busy with preparations. It would be unsatisfactory, but the telephone would have to suffice. Also Katy had decided to come a few days earlier, Patrick joining her on the Friday before the race. Allain would be coming over on the Thursday, giving him time to get the *Jonquil* ready and complete any last-minute paperwork and preparation. Betsy, Allain and Katy had planned to eat out on the Thursday night, and Betsy truly hoped that Julie and the other staff could manage without her. It was a bit of a liberty, she knew, but she was so looking forward to it. The atmosphere became increasingly frenzied, but they were a great team and the following days flew by. In any spare time she had, Betsy had her hair done, had a manicure and facial and knew she would look her best when she met Allain.

Firstly though, Katy was due to arrive. Betsy would have liked to fly to Guernsey and travel over with her, but Katy was flying direct to Alderney from Southampton. She daren't think of Katy's reaction to the flight, having refrained from telling her it would be the same tiny Trislander plane as the ones between the islands: a fourteen-seater only, no aisle and everyone having a huge picture window. The pilot would be within conversational distance. It was certainly not the experience most air passengers expected. It was noisy too, but Betsy had come to understand that, despite its being basic, it was one of the safest planes in the sky. Knowing that though wasn't always a great consolation, only continued familiarity creating confidence. Katy was probably expecting a large jet, and Betsy felt a pang of guilt at not telling her what to expect. It had been the only flight she could get; all the ones to Guernsey and even Jersey were completely full.

At the tiny airport, Katy came bustling through to where Betsy waited for her.

"You knew, didn't you? You knew I would have to fly for fifty minutes in that little tin can. Why didn't you tell me?"

"I didn't want to alarm you. Either you got on that plane or you didn't come here at all, you know that. I'm sorry – I know it is a bit of an ordeal."

"A bit of an ordeal! I nearly died of fright. I spent the whole flight with my eyes shut and my coat over my head. Never again."

Betsy stifled a laugh as she saw Katy's face green with fear and nausea.

"Don't laugh – it's not funny!"

"No, sorry, Katy. Anyway, come on – give me a hug. It's so lovely to see you. Am I forgiven?"

"I suppose so," as Katy hugged Betsy.

Betsy picked up Katy's luggage and they headed out to the car park.

"I've borrowed Henry's car again, so we don't need a taxi. Come on – get in."

Once inside, and with Betsy heading into town, Katy carried on complaining about the flight. "I'm not the only one, you know. I think lots of people were shocked about the plane. When we were all called out on to the tarmac to board there was a group of businessmen just in front. When they saw the plane they looked at each other and one of them said, 'Bloody hell, we're not flying in that, are we?'"

They both laughed.

"Well, you can't deny it's an adventure coming to Alderney, can you?" laughed Betsy.

"That's an understatement!" Katy replied. "But it's great when you do get here. You're looking great, Betsy, and you've changed your hairstyle – it suits you."

"Well, thank you. I like it too."

Katy, thankfully, wasn't the kind of person who needed to be entertained and taken everywhere. She enjoyed finding her own way around, exploring, relaxing and finding her own little adventures. This was just as well, for Betsy became increasingly busy as the week went on. Nevertheless they managed to find some quality time together and Betsy was so enjoying having Katy to keep her company, especially in the mornings before Betsy started work. They could share a leisurely breakfast, on warm mornings sitting out on the balcony, consuming large quantities of tea and coffee and catching up on news and gossip, and talking of home.

"How is my house?" asked Betsy one day, and she realised how little she had thought about it in the last weeks.

"It's fine," replied Katy, "and the garden is looking gorgeous. Ivan is doing a wonderful job for you. Some things are growing over now, but he has done such a lot of work."

"That's good to hear. I must say, one of the things I have missed is my garden," answered Betsy. "Funny, but I think I've adopted the beach and sea as a replacement. I can't wait to open the curtains each day and see how everything looks. And it does change, just like a garden. It's inspiring and reassuring too that it's always there to greet me each day. Speaking of which, do you fancy a stroll on the beach this morning? It looks lovely out there."

"I'd love that. Come on – let's go," Katy answered enthusiastically.

"I think we might go up to the next beach. We can do a bit of beachcombing and investigate the rock pools."

For the next couple of hours they enjoyed themselves just like children, with seemingly not a care in the world. They were relaxed, any worries and cares left way behind as they collected shells, pretty pebbles, bits of glass smoothed by the waves, and other interesting items too.

"This is great," shouted Katy to Betsy, who had wandered some distance away.

Betsy only just heard her. There was a strong breeze and the waves were breaking heavily on to the shore.

"Hold on – I'll come over."

Betsy sprinted across to her friend.

"Did you say how great it is?"

"I did. I feel like I'm ten years old again on my summer

holidays. Have you found anything interesting?"

"Not really, but I'm really enjoying myself. I have found a cuttlefish bone and a mermaid's purse, but no interesting flotsam or jetsam, whichever it is – I get them mixed up."

"No, I haven't found much either, but I'll take these lovely shells back, and I found a starfish and a tiny crab shell," replied Katy.

They both had red cheeks and their hair was blowing across their faces, the fresh sea air and sand stinging as it blew in their faces.

"I think it's time to head back, don't you? The wind is really getting up. The clouds are scudding across the sky and it's whipping up the sea. There are white horses out there now."

Back at the flat, cup of coffee in hand, they felt their cheeks glowing and the heat made them sleepy after the refreshing but strong wind and salty air.

"What is this life if full of care we have no time to stand and stare?" quoted Katy. "Life seems so hectic – we never seem to have time to enjoy the simple things in life. I really enjoyed that. We should do things like that more often. It's therapeutic, isn't it?"

"It is. I enjoyed it too," echoed Betsy, "and with the weekend coming on us we should chill out when we can. This literally is the lull before the storm."

By Thursday Betsy felt they were pretty well prepared. She was worried, but she was also confident that she had done as much advance work as was possible. Now she just wanted to get on with it. As the week progressed, the island became busier. It was building to a potentially huge crowd for the Saturday race. Allain confirmed he was sailing over that afternoon and Betsy couldn't wait to see him, although she knew his mind would be on the race and she did not want to distract him. She was nervous for him. She dreaded to think how he must be feeling.

Allain had been thinking the same thing. He felt terribly nervous and anxious. Realistically he knew that as a first-time entrant he had no chance of winning or even coming close, but he didn't want to be humiliated by a disappointing performance. He wanted everyone to feel proud of him and, more than that, he wanted to be proud of himself. As he edged himself around the coast and safely into harbour, he felt that more than anything he just wanted to really enjoy himself. He had left his journey late, and the sun was slowly dipping below the horizon as he prepared to moor up. On the Friday he would be allocated his formal mooring and given his entrant's number. His parents and brother were flying over on Friday too, and both he and Betsy were unsure whether or not to introduce her to them. Both concluded that another time would be more appropriate, and in truth he was relieved. The race was enough for him to concentrate his efforts on; he really didn't want to have to worry about his parents' reaction to Betsy. It was selfish, he knew, but it was the only way he would ensure all his concentration was purely on the race.

Betsy and Katy had agreed to meet Allain in the tiny Italian restaurant at the far end of town. He had called to say he would be later than expected and they should eat. By the time he eventually arrived they had almost finished their meal.

"Oh, here he is now!" Betsy exclaimed, unable to keep the relief out of her voice.

Allain rushed to their table.

"We'd almost given up on you. Is everything OK?"

"I'm really sorry, and, Katy, what must you think of me?" apologised Allain.

Katy replied, laughing, "Don't worry – everything is fine. We've had a good chat over the meal and it means we can stay a bit longer and share some more wine with you. Anyway, it's good to meet you again."

"And you, and I'm looking forward to meeting your husband – Patrick, isn't it? Is it tomorrow he arrives?"

"Yes, about lunchtime," confirmed Katy.

Allain then looked over to Betsy and moved to give her a kiss.

"It's so good to see you. It seems ages since I last saw you. You look lovely, Betsy – radiant – and you've changed your hairstyle. It suits you."

They looked into each other's eyes, smouldering and passionate. He wasn't making it up – she could tell he really was pleased to see her.

"Now come – sit down and order some food. You must be starving. We just had pizza and salad, but it was tasty," Betsy told him.

"I'll have the same, then."

"In that case, Katy and I will just have to have a dessert. We can't let you eat on your own. What do you say, Katy?"

"Definitely. I mean, we don't really want a huge helping of ice cream, but we'll have to eat something."

They all laughed and then relaxed, and all three knew they would enjoy the rest of the evening.

It was the early hours before they set off back, and it was a clear moonlit night, full of stars. The night air was warm, balmy even – the kind of night when you don't want to go in, but sit and enjoy. When they reached the harbour, Katy left and returned to the bistro, giving both Betsy and Allain a hug and kiss before parting.

"Night, you two. See you in the morning."

Allain and Betsy continued walking hand in hand on down

to the harbour and jetty, where the *Jonquil* was rocking gently in the water. It was incredibly quiet, and they spoke in hushed tones, not wanting to disturb the tranquil night. Near the *Jonquil* they both stood on the quayside, both silently soaking up the atmosphere of the beautiful night.

"It is so gorgeous, Allain. The sky is full of stars and the moon is so clear, the moonbeams reflecting on the water. I can't remember when I last felt so happy. How lucky am I to be in such an amazing place with the most amazing man in the world!"

"Do I really make you happy, Betsy?"

"Yes, you do. I love you, Allain."

"I love you too, Betsy. I really do love you."

Then he took her in his arms and under the array of twinkling stars he kissed her, holding her like he would never let her go.

"Would you like to sleep on the boat with me tonight?"

"I think you already know the answer to that."

And they both walked along the pontoon and disappeared into the small berth. Betsy lay on the bed while Allain made coffee. Then, later, as they lay in bed together and made love, Betsy thought she would cry with happiness. Allain quickly fell into a deep sleep, but despite her tiredness Betsy lay awake, the gentle rocking of the boat and the lapping of the waves on the boat sides relaxing her and comforting her. She wanted to continue experiencing the wonderful feeling and the knowledge that her life would never be the same again. The happiness she had never expected had returned sevenfold so that she could hardly contain it or even believe it.

'Thank You, God, thank You.'

And she finally fell into a deep untroubled sleep.

They enjoyed an early breakfast together the next morning and then Allain accompanied Betsy back up to the bistro. She was preparing for a busy day and they would have little time to spend together. Allain was spending some time at the yacht club and was then meeting his family at the airport.

"I'll call in and let you know my race number, but other than that I think it might be race day before I see you."

"Yes, don't worry – spend some time with your parents, have an early night and I'll see you in the morning. I'll walk down very early and we can have coffee together."

"OK, then, have a good day. Give me a kiss and I'll see you as soon as I can."

They hugged and kissed and then Betsy stood by the door to the bistro and waved as he walked off towards the yacht club. He turned and waved back, Betsy then going inside to turn her mind to her staff and customers, gearing up for a busy but exciting day and night.

The build-up was rapid. People were arriving constantly, wandering round, enjoying the anticipation and atmosphere, looking forward to the next day and a hopefully exciting race. Preparations were taking place down at the harbour too, bunting being strung and staging going up along with a small quantity of grandstand seating for special guests. Other vantage points would be all along the sea wall and the quayside and even up along the cliffs, where people would be taking picnics and looking out to sea at the same time. It looked set to be an exciting day.

Hectic it certainly was. Betsy didn't have time to miss Allain. Her feet hardly touched the ground, and she was grateful that Katy understood the situation. Katy met Patrick at the airport and spent the rest of the day showing him around, relaxing and watching the arrangements taking place down at the harbour. The atmosphere was electric and palpable. Betsy looked frazzled when they got to the bistro.

"I take it you've been busy, then," Katy teased her, then gave her a hug.

"You could say that, but it has kept my mind away from the race. Patrick, it is so lovely to see you." And she walked over and gave him a big hug and kiss. "How was the flight? Full, I expect."

"It was fine," returned Patrick, "and I must say Alderney is nothing like what I imagined. It's gorgeous and the atmosphere is fabulous. I can't wait for tomorrow."

"I'm so glad you could come. Now I need to get back to our customers, but why don't you bring in your luggage and I'll join you later? Are you going to eat here?"

"If you can fit us in we will," Katy replied.

"You won't mind if I don't join you, and honestly I am so exhausted."

"You do look tired. Don't worry – we'll do our own thing and see you in the morning for the main event," Katy said reassuringly.

"Come on, then, Katy," said Patrick. "Let's go and sort out my luggage, and let Betsy get on."

Just as Patrick was picking up his case and heading up to the flat, Katy shouted out, "Allain, oh, hi. It's great to see you. Is everything OK?"

"No problem. I just told Betsy I would call and let her know my berthing number. Now this must be Patrick?" And Allain headed over to him to shake his hand. "Glad to meet you. We'll have to get together after the race and we can have a drink."

"That would be great. I'll look forward to it."

"Oh, here's Betsy, coming out of the kitchen. She looks tired."

"Yes, she's had a really busy day and it isn't over yet," confirmed Katy.

Then Betsy saw him and her eyes lit up, she was so pleased to see him.

"Can you spare a minute?" Allain asked.

"'Course. Come on – we'll go out on to the terrace for a while. Do you want a drink?"

"No, no. I need to get back to Mum and Dad and James – they're waiting for me over at the yacht club. But I wanted to see you and let you know where my berth will be."

"Have you had a good day with your parents?"

"I have. They've really enjoyed it. The day has passed really quickly and it's stopped me worrying too much."

"I'm so glad. Hope they enjoy it tomorrow."

He said farewell to Betsy, who watched him as he set off to meet his parents and hopefully eat something, if his nerves would allow.

'Oh, I love him so much.' And she felt her stomach full of butterflies. 'Take care tomorrow,' she said to herself.

Betsy went late to bed, by which time Allain had already retired. He thought an early night would help to calm him, relax him, give him a good sleep to waken refreshed for an early start, preparing for the most important sail of his life. But sleep was a distant companion. However hard he tried, sleep eluded him.

He tossed and turned, he was hot, uncomfortable, and he eventually got up, went on deck to take some air, poured himself a large whisky and tried to compose himself. The day he had been planning for so long was now almost here.

'Let me enjoy it. Let me do my best. Let Betsy be proud of me. Please don't let Francesca turn up. Don't let anything spoil the day.'

After so much planning and excitement he couldn't stand that. His family hadn't mentioned her, so he didn't know whether or not she planned to come. His parents knew something wasn't right with them, but thankfully they said nothing. They too knew it was important that Allain had no uncomfortable distractions.

And finally, as he sat and the night air grew cool, he felt his eyes droop. He went back down to the berth, got into bed and immediately fell into a heavy sleep. Next time he woke, the day of the race would finally have arrived. It would be a momentous day.

Chapter Eight

It was like a carnival day. From early morning people had been congregating around the harbour. It was like Ladies Day at the races, with women dressed in beautiful dresses, high heels and enormous hats. There were families too, the children excitable, local children spotting their friends and running off to meet them. Most of the preparations had been completed – the bunting fluttered in the breeze, microphones for the race commentary were being tested.

Special guests started to arrive though it was still early. Even though the race wouldn't begin for a few hours, everyone wanted to make the most of the day. A band was playing on the quayside, ice cream was for sale, there were stalls selling everything from local crafts and home-made cakes to dinghies and yachts, there was a bouncy castle for the children and a couple of fairground rides, and the lifeboat was giving tours around the harbour. All in all it was the start of what was going to be a very special day. The most important people too were there – the sailors and their yachts, berthed, ready and waiting to sail. It was certainly a wonderful sight. There were thirty entrants in all, and their immaculate vessels rocked gently, their sails and pennants fluttering, each name and number standing out clearly. Visitors walked up and down the quayside looking at all the boats, commenting on the names, such as *Paper Moon*, *Bellissimo*, *Moonlight* and *Wild Water*, and the size and luxuriousness of the various yachts. People would point to those which made a big impression, or maybe they knew their owners. Also the owners – some seasoned entrants, including some former winners, and some newcomers like Allain – were waiting, knowing that there was little time for more preparation and there was no backing out. This was what it had all been for. Allain, like all the others, knew that now it would be him, his yacht and the sea. No gimmicks, just skill, determination and the desperate will to win.

Allain and Betsy had taken breakfast together, and when she had left him to open the bistro he was calm. He was going to spend a little time with his parents too, and then Betsy would come to see him just before the start. She knew the bistro would empty at that point as everyone would head down towards the harbour to try and find a good vantage point.

Katy and Patrick appeared in the bistro.

"Well, look at you two! Talk about looking perfect for the occasion."

Patrick was perfect in his chinos and polo shirt while Katy wore a flowing maxi dress in a vibrant yellow.

"I know, and we're off now to have a wander around. Shall we see you near Allain's berth just before the start?"

"Yes, I'll try and get away as soon as it gets a bit quiet in here."

She was obviously showing her support for the *Jonquil*.

"How was he this morning?" asked Katy of Allain's state of mind.

"Actually he was remarkably calm. Said he'd slept well, which is good. He's worried Francesca will arrive though, make a scene and spoil the whole thing."

"Oh, I hope not. I hadn't thought about that," Katy replied, her voice full of concern.

"I doubt she will," Betsy commented confidently. "Even *she* wouldn't spoil Allain's chance of winning. At least I hope she won't. Well, go on – off you go. Enjoy yourselves."

"We will," answered Patrick, "and make sure you get away – you don't want to miss the start."

"Oh, I couldn't possibly miss it, and I can't miss the end either. I need to see Allain getting the winner's trophy!"

"Do you really think he'll win?" Patrick asked.

"No, Patrick, it's wishful thinking. There is an awful lot of competition out there, and I agree with Allain that if he finishes without disgracing himself he'll feel happy."

"Oh, Betsy, it's so exciting," Katy continued. "You wouldn't think – would you? – that it was simply an insignificant little island race. I feel as nervous and excited for him as if he was attempting a world record. And I'm still going to bet on him to win. Is there going to be some kind of Tote?"

"I believe so – an official thing, with a temporary office somewhere on the harbour – but I haven't seen it. But please don't call it an insignificant little race – the locals will banish you for heresy. How could you, Katy?"

And they both laughed.

"Don't worry – we'll find it. Now, try not to wear yourself out and we'll see you later."

Betsy watched them disappear down the road and waved to them. Then she turned her attention to her many customers, and checked to see that her staff were coping. They were, and she settled into her work routine, looking forward to the start of the race and seeing Allain set off.

The weather had changed. It was still dry and warm, but the air was heavy and sticky, the sky was overcast and it felt oppressive. It wasn't the best weather for sailing, but at least the sea was calm. A slight freshening breeze would be welcome, and Betsy knew Allain, like everyone else, would be hoping the rain held off. But there was no point in worrying about that – one thing you couldn't control was the weather.

Allain's earlier calm was evaporating as the hours before the race seemed to drag. He just wanted to get on with it. There was absolutely nothing more he could do, and sitting and just pottering about was making him irritable. But his spirits lifted as he saw his parents and brother approaching.

"Hi. I'm so glad to see you. I'm going stir-crazy here trying to pass the time."

"Hello, sweetheart," said his mother as she stepped on board and gave him a hug.

His father and brother followed, his father shaking his hand – a formal gesture, for he was nervous too.

"Are you all prepared, then? Is there anything we can do?" queried his mother.

"Not here, no. There is really absolutely nothing more I can do. I've checked and checked. I actually need to get away for a while. Do you fancy going for a drink? It would help me calm down a bit."

So no sooner had they arrived than they were all heading back along the harbour, where they sat listening to the band. Allain's father walked to one of the temporary kiosks and returned with paper cups of tea and coffee for everyone.

"I can't believe how busy it is," James said. "We're lucky to even find a seat. And there is so much going on and so many people to watch. It'll take your mind off things for a while, Allain."

"It will. I feel better already. I was starting to feel a bit panicky there on my own, sweating and agitated. I hope you enjoy it, all of you; are you going to have a little bet?"

"'Course we are. Have they announced any odds yet?"

"Don't know, but I'll have very long odds – you know that, don't you? I'm one of the least experienced in the race."

"It doesn't matter," replied his father. "You are a brilliant yachtsman – you know that. We have every confidence in you, son. It doesn't matter what the odds are – we'll still be betting on you. And when you win we'll make a lot of money, won't we, James?"

"We certainly will," James agreed.

"Thanks. I'll do my best. I love you all. Thanks for all your support."

Time had crept by and then it suddenly seemed to speed up and Allain felt he ought to get back for his final preparation. They all walked quietly together back with him. They left him at the berth. Allain jumped on to his yacht and his family bade him a last farewell.

"Have you got the tickets I got for you?" Allain said, suddenly remembering. "Entrants' families can have reserved places. You should get a good spot to see me leave."

"Don't worry – we've got them," his mother shouted to him. "We'll see you later. Good luck, darling, and enjoy yourself."

Then they were gone, and Allain was once more alone. He decided to freshen up and change, then he was as ready as he could be, and he continually looked anxiously at his watch. Not long to go now.

At the bistro Betsy was also starting to feel somewhat anxious. The customers weren't leaving as fast as she would have liked. They were boisterous and she wished they would quickly eat and drink up and leave. Then finally, as they realised the time, they dispersed and Betsy and her staff gave a great sigh of relief.

"OK, everyone, let's close up until the race is under way. We'll go and join all the fun."

Betsy left them at the harbour, where the crowd seemed to have increased further and the atmosphere had gathered momentum. She knew time was running out and she couldn't wait to spend some final minutes with Allain. As she approached his yacht she saw him on deck, and at that moment he took her breath away. He hadn't seen her and he looked so full of concentration, so serious. He was dressed to match his boat, in white shorts, a yellow guernsey, white deck shoes and a hat. Betsy couldn't believe how handsome he looked, and she felt she loved him dreadfully at that moment. She stood and just looked at him, feeling happy and very, very lucky. How had she managed to find such a wonderful man? she wondered. Then he saw her and waved, and his serious countenance was at once transformed, happy and smiling, welcoming her excitedly on board.

"Oh, I have been waiting to see you all day. I feel so much better now you are here," he said as he held her and kissed her.

"I know. I'm sorry I took so long – I thought the customers would never go. But I couldn't wait to see you. Are you all set? Do you think the weather will hold?" asked Betsy.

"I hope so, but it's so humid I won't be surprised if we have a thunderstorm."

"That would be a bit of a disaster, wouldn't it?"

"Not the best conditions, no, but a bit of rain is better than a gale. We'll have to see."

"I suppose so," agreed Betsy. "By the way, have you seen Katy and Patrick? We said we'd meet up here so they can wish you luck."

"I haven't seen them, no."

"Well, they're cutting it a bit fine, aren't they? Oh, here

they are, look. Hi there! Thought you might be too late. Come on board."

"Sorry we took so long, but we couldn't not come and wish you luck," apologised Katy.

Then she hugged Allain, and Patrick shook his hand.

"Brave man, Allain," announced Patrick. "Hope you do well."

"Thanks," replied Allain. "I hope I do too."

"Short and sweet," said Katy, "but we'll leave you now and see if we can find a good viewing point. See you up there, Betsy." Then in an aside so Allain couldn't hear she asked Betsy, "No sign of you-know-who, then?"

"No," said a relieved Betsy. "It looks like I was right: I don't think she is anywhere on the island, thank goodness."

Then Betsy too was back on the quayside, having found Katy and Patrick with difficulty. The band had stopped playing and the commentator approached the microphone.

"Ladies, gentlemen, distinguished guests, welcome to Alderney's St Anne Challenge. It has been a long morning's wait, but shortly we will see the thirty yachts entered into this year's race begin their sail out of the harbour ready to begin. They will be led out in number order by the previous race winner, Raymond de Villiers of Jersey, sailing his former winning yacht, *Jersey Pride*. And here he comes now, so let's hear a round of applause for our reigning champion."

There was a huge round of applause and everyone shouted, eager and excited to see the race begin. Then all the other yachts came into formation and followed out towards the harbour mouth. At this point the band started to play again, some people blew whistles, others beat drums, and everyone else clapped and shouted, enjoying the spectacle of the beautiful yachts sailing past all the spectators and out into the sea.

"There's Allain," shouted Betsy to Katy. "He looks wonderful and the *Jonquil* looks so sturdy and proud."

"I can see him," Katy answered.

"Oh, good luck, Allain, good luck."

Then all the yachts had left, and a flotilla of other small boats and dinghies followed them out to encourage them on their way, and in a short time the foghorn from the lighthouse sounded three times – the signal for the race to commence.

"And they are off," said the commentator excitedly. "Good luck, everyone, and we look forward to seeing who will be in the lead after the first circuit of the island."

There was little breeze at the start and the yachts struggled to get up much speed, but gradually they all sailed away until they had disappeared around the first turn of the island. Those without clifftop viewpoints started to disperse, intending to return at a later stage. Those high up on the cliffs stood watching and waving as they had a longer and wider view of the yachts as they rounded the cliffs and made their first attempt to take an early lead. Then they relaxed on to the tussocky grass and opened their picnic baskets, relaxing and waiting for another view as the yachts rounded the island.

Back in town Betsy, Katy and Patrick were relieved that everything had gone well. They knew that all they could do was wait and hope that Allain would hold his own with all the others. He had prepared so hard that Betsy felt he deserved to complete the race. She felt so proud of him.

"I'm going to have to go back to the bistro for a while," Betsy said to Katy and Patrick. "It won't be overly busy, I imagine. Most people will hang around here. At the end of the race though, I expect quite an onslaught. It's hard to know really. What are you two planning?"

"Oh, we're going to just hang around, soaking up the

atmosphere. We're hoping to go out on the lifeboat, have a few drinks. . . . You know."

"Oh, I know. Wish I could join you, but some of us have to work!"

"Oh, you poor thing!" Katy laughed. "Shall we come and tell you what's happening?"

"Oh, please," answered Betsy. "I can hear the commentator from out on the terrace, but it won't be very clear. I feel so nervous for Allain. I'm almost glad to be working, to take my mind off everything. See you later, then. Enjoy yourselves."

"We will, we are," Patrick rejoined, and waved as Betsy headed off.

"I know we have the commentary, but it's strange not to be able to see what's happening, isn't it, Patrick?"

"It is a bit, but I don't suppose it's that different to a horse race when you can't get a view of the winning post," answered Patrick. "Anyhow, let's hope all is going well and we can go and enjoy ourselves."

"That sounds good to me."

The weather stayed dry, but it also continued sticky and heavy and Katy hoped there was a better breeze out at sea than on dry land. The air felt uncomfortable and draining, but at least it was dry.

There were no problems with any of the yachts and the master of ceremonies was preparing to announce the early leader. The time had passed sooner than Katy expected and she was eager to hear the report.

"Well, everyone," the commentator began, "despite the heavy weather the yachts have made good progress. There has been a good headwind and we can now see the first yachts approaching around the headland. In fact, now I think we are able to see the early leader. And it is number 7, Michel Gutierrez from Boulogne, sailing *Mon Ami*, and he is closely followed by David de l'Isle of Guernsey with *Fermaine*. All the others look to be following close at their heels. So let's see if these two can hold their lead. It's early days yet and, as the saying goes, anything can happen."

Katy related the early placing to Betsy, who was busy but not overly so. Then she and Patrick set off to enjoy a trip on the lifeboat. It was a short sail, but an interesting one, learning how many people it had rescued from the treacherous Alderney waters. Most of the crew doubled as fishermen, but there were also landlords, plumbers and even teachers.

Betsy kept a keen watch on the weather. She was sure it would break, and sure enough as the race progressed to its climax she heard some distant rumbles of thunder. She was unsure whether this was good or not. Certainly some rain would clear the air – everyone, including the yachtsmen, would feel more comfortable – but she knew from what Allain had told her that rain hampered progress. The harder it rained the harder it would be. Heavy rain with accompanying wind is not congenial to sailing. Then it started to rain. It thundered, and then came lightning and thunder, and heavier rain. People piled into the bistro, abandoning the harbourside even though the race was drawing to a close. It couldn't be a worse finale. She felt acutely for Allain and indeed everyone else. Nevertheless, after drying out, most customers, having acquired umbrellas, made their way back. Whatever the weather, they were not going to miss the final moments of the race. Nor was Betsy. She and her staff politely ushered out her customers and headed along to the harbour with them. Most people were at least a little bit soggy, but knew they wouldn't have to wait much longer in the rain. The commentator was gearing up for the end too.

"The scouts tell me that the first yachts are about to round the final headland now. So hold on to your hats –

or more likely your umbrellas – as we prepare to welcome the winner of this year's St Anne Challenge. Despite the rain it has been an enormous success. Everyone, I hope, has enjoyed the day, and I know that a great deal of money has been raised for the Alderney lifeboat. Thank you, everyone, for your generosity. And now I can announce the leaders as they approach the harbour."

At that moment there was an enormous crash of thunder and a massive squally wind took hold. Out in the bay as the yachts approached the sea began to boil. Waves rose, and the swell too. It looked dangerous out there. Thankfully most yachts were approaching a safe haven. It would be only minutes now before the winners would emerge, weather-beaten and exhausted but hopefully all intact.

"And now let's get them all inshore," said the commentator. "It's been a great sail, but we'd like to see them all home safe, if not dry. And here now we can see our leaders. Coming in now we have, in first place, number 11, Roman Lascalles, from St Malo with *Mignonette*. In second place, which he has kept right through, is David de l'Isle of Guernsey. Now we can see, coming up in third place, number 22, Catriona Wesley from Jersey, with her lovely little yacht, *Egret*. Then coming up fast, but unable to catch her, in a very close fourth place is Allain Laubert of Guernsey with the *Jonquil*, number 19 – a brilliant sail for Allain in his first ever challenge. Well done, everyone. Now don't desert us in the rain – we want a rapturous welcome back, not only for our winner, but for all the entrants. We might be a small island, but this is a big Challenge."

On the harbourside, having found Katy and Patrick, Betsy was ecstatic. "I just can't believe it, Katy. Fourth! He's come fourth. It's a brilliant achievement."

And she and Katy, like a couple of children, held hands and danced around in a circle. Betsy had been confident he would finish, but she never imagined he would be up amongst the leaders.

"Do you know, I don't care about the rain now; I just want to wait here and watch him come sailing proudly into the harbour. Oh, how wonderful he must be feeling!"

The crowd had inevitably thinned out, but there were still many people left, cheering and shouting as the winner sailed into the harbour. Betsy, Katy and Patrick found a spot right at the edge of the quayside and eagerly awaited not just Allain, but all of the skilled yachtsmen and women. Yachts trickled in and then came in thick and fast. The foghorn at the lighthouse sounded loudly to welcome them.

"I can't see him, Katy, can you?"

"He should be well in view now. Others who were behind him are already here and getting ready to moor up. The presentation will be taking place soon. What's he doing?"

"I can't see him either, but it is a bit chaotic out there," said Katy, herself feeling equally confused.

"I'll go and walk around," Patrick said. "We may have just missed him – easy to do with all this going on."

"I'm coming too," announced Betsy.

"Me too," added Katy.

They walked around and around, but however hard they looked they could not see Allain or his yacht. His allocated berth was empty and Betsy felt a rising panic.

"There's something wrong – there must be. He should have moored up long ago. Everyone else is here. Something has happened."

"No, Betsy, he was here at the finish – you know that. They announced him. He must be somewhere. Don't worry – we'll find him."

"No, Katy, I know. Come on – we've got to find out."

They headed urgently for the commentator's stand, but it was empty. Arrangements were obviously being made for the presentations. Then Betsy turned back to the water and saw the lifeboat heading out.

"Look, Katy – the lifeboat. It's heading out and it doesn't look like a practice or a pleasure trip."

"How do you know? Please don't panic, Betsy, please."

"Oh my God, Katy, it's Allain, I'm sure of it. What can have happened? I can't bear it – I need to know." She burst into tears and Katy hugged her and guided her away in the direction of the bistro.

"No, Katy, I need to stay here. I need to find out."

But it was impossible to find out. People were milling about, but whom should she ask?

"Come on – let me take you back. Patrick can see if he can find out anything."

Reluctantly Betsy let Katy escort her back to the bistro. Patrick stayed and made endless enquiries, but however hard he tried he couldn't discover anything. He asked in the first-aid tent and he asked at the lifeboat shop, but people wherever he went either couldn't or wouldn't tell him anything.

In the meantime Katy had managed to get Betsy into the bistro, where she accepted a large whisky. It settled her, but she didn't feel any better. She then began to shiver and the tears flowed. She just didn't know what to do.

Patrick returned. Katy turned to him quickly, but he simply shook his head.

"Is there any news, Patrick?" Betsy whispered, struggling to speak through her tears.

"I don't know. I can't find out anything. No one will speak to me, but I genuinely don't think anyone knows. There is an atmosphere though. Something is wrong – I think we need to accept that, Betsy."

"No," Betsy wailed. "He's dead – he must be dead. There's no other explanation, is there?"

"We don't know that, Betsy," Katy comforted. "We'll find out, but please don't think the worst."

Betsy was sitting in a corner, and fortunately there were few customers. The rain had sent people home, and others had been asked politely if they would leave as soon as possible. It was clear a tragedy was unfolding.

The weather was still atrocious, but the rain had eased a little. The sky was dark and menacing, but it looked like the rain might stop soon. Not that that helped any. The awards ceremony had been diverted to the yacht club, and the harbourside was rapidly emptying. Everywhere looked forlorn, and what had been an exciting day had turned into a nightmare.

Then there was the sound of propellers. A helicopter was on its way. Patrick leapt up and dashed out back down to the harbour. The helicopter, an air ambulance, was coming in to land and at the quayside was the lifeboat. Patrick was not allowed near – he was told politely to leave the area. He did so, but not before he heard a conversation.

"We are his parents. Will it be possible for us to come in the helicopter with him?"

"Of course – they are bringing him now."

Patrick walked slowly back. He felt unable to face Betsy. It seemed she was right: Allain was, he thought, being airlifted back to Guernsey. But was he dead or alive?

Betsy heard Patrick's news calmly. After all, it was only what she had imagined all the time. Allain was dead. He must be. There could be no other explanation for all the mystery and silence.

"Come on, Betsy – we need to get you into the flat. There's nothing you can do here now. We can only wait and see what news there is."

Betsy stood up weakly and fainted in Katy's arms.

Julie all this time had been watching and doing what she

could. When Katy eventually managed to get Betsy out of the bistro, Julie spoke to Patrick.

"Patrick, I can find out what has happened. I have a relative who works for the air ambulance. It's all supposed to be confidential, but he'll tell me if I explain. It may take a few hours to get hold of him, but I'll find out, I promise."

"Thanks, Julie. At least then we will know one way or another."

"Yes," said Julie, her voice choked with tears, "we will. Pray it is not what we think."

Chapter Nine

It is an understatement to say they all spent a troubled sleepless night. As dawn broke it was still damp, dismal, chilly and overcast.

"A bit like our mood, Patrick, this weather, isn't it? I can barely face today – I shudder to think how Betsy must be. Oh, Patrick, it is so awful."

Patrick moved to the bedroom window and hugged his wife.

"Not knowing doesn't help, does it?" he said. "I wonder how Julie is getting on. If we don't hear from her soon, I'm going to ring the hospitals and police again. I'll make someone tell me something."

Betsy felt unable to get out of bed. What was the point? She didn't want to face anyone, and there was nothing to get up for. She hoped it had all been a dream, but she knew it was real. She was exhausted from crying, anxiety, no sleep or food, and she was content to lie and let the world carry on around her. Katy emerged from the kitchen.

"I've brought you some tea," announced Katy. "Try and drink it – you need to have something."

"Is there any news?"

"No, we'll tell you as soon as we hear. I'm sure Julie or Patrick will find out soon. We'll contact Allain's parents if we have to."

Betsy, after a few sips of tea, fell back on to the pillow. The sofa bed was normally so uncomfortable that a lie-in was not a temptation. This morning, Betsy, immune to its discomfort, closed her eyes trying desperately to blot out the unbearable feeling of pain and almost terror at the thought of Allain being dead.

"Please, God," she prayed in earnest, "please don't let him be dead. I'll do anything You want, but let him be alive." And tears streamed down her face, endless hot tears, which burned her cheeks and ran into her mouth, salty and bitter.

It was frustrating for Julie too. What she thought would be a relatively easy task was proving to be the opposite. She knew her brother-in-law had not been on duty at the time of the accident, but when she spoke to him and explained the situation he said not to worry. He told her he would make enquiries and come back to her as soon as he could. Several hours later information was still in short supply.

"What's the problem, Steve?" she asked when he phoned her.

"Well, the pilot from yesterday went off duty as soon as he came back to Guernsey. He's now gone off on holiday, so I can't speak to him."

"What about the co-pilot? Does he not know?"

"*She* – the co-pilot is a *she*, and as she's off duty too we can't get hold of her."

"Oh, Steve, there must be something we can do!"

"Don't worry – of course there is. It's just taking a bit longer, that's all," comforted Steve. "A report would have been filed and I'm just waiting now for someone to get hold of it for me. I'm not meant to tell you about it, Julie, so I can't rush them, can I? Just give me a while. I'll come back to you."

So the waiting continued, the time dragging unbearably, everyone edgy, creeping around, conversation muted. Betsy, having forced herself out of bed, sat slumped in a chair, her eyes closed. She was awake, though wishing she wasn't. What was happening at the bistro she neither knew nor cared. Katy and Patrick, at a total loss as to how to help Betsy, had retreated to the kitchen, sitting at the table, minds blank, eyes adrift.

"If Julie doesn't ring in the next half-hour we'll ring her, OK?" Katy said to Patrick.

"Yes, OK, and if she can't find out anything then I'm going to find out myself somehow."

They both lapsed into an uncomfortable silence, Katy staring at the telephone, willing Julie to ring. Then a couple of minutes later it did.

"You take it, Katy."

And she picked it up. It was Julie.

"Katy, I'm so sorry I've taken so long getting back to you."

"It's OK, Julie. Just tell me what you know," replied an agitated Katy.

"He's alive, Katy, he's alive."

Katy almost dropped the telephone with relief. "Thank God." She gestured to Patrick with a thumbs up and mouthed to him to go and tell Betsy.

"That's the good news, Katy, but he is in a critical condition, in a coma with severe head injuries."

"Oh, no, no, Julie. Do you know what happened?"

"Not exactly, but Steve said that in the report the lifeboat was summoned when the storm broke. They think the heavy squall and wind knocked Allain off balance. He fell overboard just as he was heading for the harbour, and got trapped and injured under the boat. He was lucky not to have drowned. When the lifeboatmen found him he

115

was unconscious, and they thought he wasn't going to make it. The helicopter took him straight to the hospital on Guernsey, where I assume he will remain unless they decide to transfer him to a more specialist hospital. But he hadn't regained consciousness when they left him. It doesn't sound good, but he is still alive."

"Oh, Julie, I can't believe this has happened."

"No, I know. It's awful, isn't it? How is Betsy?"

"Calm actually, but in an awful state. So shall we phone the hospital? Will they tell us anything, do you think?"

"I'd certainly try. Say some close friends want to know his condition. Let me know how you get on, won't you? I'm not opening the bistro – would you put a notice on the door for me?"

"'Course, no problem. And, Julie, thank you so much for finding out for us. I don't know what we would have done without you. I must go now – I can hear Betsy and Patrick. I need to tell them. Thanks again. Bye, Julie."

"Katy, what's happening?" shouted a panicky but excited Betsy. "Is it true? Is he alive?"

Katy went into the living room, where two pairs of desperate eyes were awaiting the news. Katy went over to hug Betsy.

"He is alive, Betsy. He is, but he is very poorly. He had a terrible accident."

She told them both the rest and watched the colour drain from Betsy's face as her earlier optimism evaporated.

"A coma? Unconscious? Oh, my poor darling Allain!" And she was once more overcome with grief.

"But the main thing is that he is alive and there is hope of recovery. That's right, isn't it, Patrick?"

"Katy is right, Betsy. It might be a long haul for him, but let's be positive. And you know you can help him, can't you?" Patrick replied encouragingly.

"You're right," agreed Betsy. "Of course you're right. I must go and see him right away."

"Well, not right away, Betsy. You aren't strong enough, and we need to find out definitely where he is. Stay here. Patrick and I will make some calls and we'll go up to the airport to see if we can get a flight for tomorrow."

"No, I need to go – I need to go now!" exclaimed Betsy.

"No, Betsy, I know how desperate you are, but please let us organise things for you."

"OK, Katy, you're right. At least I know he is still alive."

"Now Patrick and I will need to leave you for a while. Are you going to be OK? Do you want me to ask Julie to come over?"

"I'll be fine, really."

"Are you sure?"

"I'm sure – I'll be all right."

"Well, I'm going to put the radio on – there may be something on the local news."

"Do you think so? Yes, it might tell us a little. It's doubtful though – hospitals never like to divulge much. They probably won't tell *us* anything either."

"It's worth a try," insisted Katy and she brought the radio in from the kitchen.

They listened to the news and nothing seemed to be forthcoming. Katy was about to switch it off when the announcer continued: "Now the Channel Island sports news and first news of the tragedy. Alderney's St Anne Challenge was yesterday marred by tragedy. In adverse weather towards the very end of the yacht race Guernsey yachtsman Allain Laubert, a first-time entrant but an experienced sailor, was seriously injured when he was washed overboard. He was rescued by the lifeboat and then taken by helicopter to hospital on Guernsey. He is understood to have sustained severe head injuries. He is currently in a critical but stable condition, says a hospital spokesperson. We wish Allain a speedy recovery and send our best wishes to his family, who are said to be maintaining a bedside vigil. Now other sports news and we turn to the inter-island cricket tournament. . . ."

Katy switched off the radio and looked at Betsy, whose eyes were glistening both with tears and with hope.

"So can we please go tomorrow – please, Katy?"

Both Katy and Patrick were glad to be out of doors.

"I needed this fresh air," said Patrick. "The atmosphere was so tense and overpowering there. So what are we planning to do, Katy? Here we are with Betsy totally unable to cope and we were due to go home tomorrow."

They had set off up the main street, which was quite deserted, a steady drizzle falling from a leaden sky.

"I don't know, Patrick, but if we can get to the hospital tomorrow we'll see how Betsy is and maybe we can still get home."

Patrick gave her a withering look. "You know that isn't likely."

"You're right, so you go back and I'll have to take a couple of extra days. It'll be fine."

"That sounds like a plan. So for now shall we get up to the airport and see if we can all get over there? We do now know he's on Guernsey and is likely to be in intensive care. We'll just go there – they can only send us away, but they probably won't."

The next day Betsy seemed transformed. She had regained her strength and fortitude. Though still pale, she was dry-eyed, and was quite overactive as she tried hard to cope with her overwhelming anxiety. She knew she was on her way to see Allain and she was eager to go. However terrible

118

the situation might be, he was alive. Just to see him would make her feel better.

They hadn't needed to worry about seats – the plane was almost empty. The weather had improved slightly – grey sky, but dry and clear. On the short flight they could see a few boats on the sea below, and the sea was calm but a sludgy grey. In no time at all they saw Guernsey ahead. So often it was like a glittering jewel in the sea; today, like their mood, it seemed flat and uninspiring.

Outside the small terminal they sought out a taxi. Betsy felt faint and weak. Even such a short journey had exhausted her. Katy had admired her efforts earlier, when she tried hard to look and feel normal. Her efforts had only partly succeeded. She was pale and grey, and despite her bravado Katy knew she was very frightened. Her heart ached for her friend. They did not know what to expect. Allain might have died overnight – something none of them had dared to mention, yet all three knew it was a real possibility.

"St Peter Port, please," Patrick said to the driver as all three got into the taxi.

"But the hospital is out of town, isn't it?" questioned Betsy.

"We're going to go and get a drink first. You need a rest and a breathing space, Betsy. Then we'll head up to the hospital," Patrick told her.

Betsy knew Patrick was right, and the refreshment did restore her a little. But she was impatient and desperately wanted to carry on.

The hospital, by town and city standards, was small, but it was new, with gleaming glass. Like most hospitals it didn't seem particularly welcoming, but seemed efficient and reassuring.

"We never checked visiting times!" exclaimed Betsy, suddenly concerned they might be faced with a long wait.

"It'll be all right," reassured Katy. "I don't think it applies to intensive care."

Approaching the lift, they looked at the information boards. Intensive care was on the fourth floor. Stepping out of the lift on to the ward, they were struck by the silence and the subdued lighting.

"It's a bit eerie," Katy whispered to Patrick. "It makes me want to whisper and creep along in case my footsteps cause some disturbance."

At the very entrance to the ward the doors were closed and some chairs were arranged in a line against the wall.

"Let's sit here for a minute, Betsy, and we can decide what we are going to do."

So all three sat with Betsy, perched uncomfortably on the edge of their chairs, edgy and slightly panicky.

"Suppose I go up to the nurses' station and ask about Allain for you?" suggested Katy. "And if we can go in and see him, do you want to go alone or shall I come with you?"

"I'd be grateful if you could find out for me, but then I think I might go in just on my own."

"OK, wait here for a minute, then." And Katy grasped Betsy's hand reassuringly as she passed.

Betsy waited quietly, but, inside, her emotions were anything but quiet. She felt sick with worry. 'Please, God, he's still here and alive,' she said to herself.

Then Katy returned, her face showing relief and the shadow of a smile. She held both of Betsy's hands and looked gently at her.

"They wouldn't tell me much, sweetheart, because I'm not close family, but they did confirm that he is still here, though still in a critical condition."

"So will they let me in, do you think?"

"I told them you were his fiancée and had only just managed to get here. The Nurse seemed perplexed. She said she thought his fiancée, Miss Duvall, was already here, with his family. No, I corrected her."

"So Francesca is here! I should have known. Oh, Katy, I'm not sure I can face going in there."

"Oh, yes, you can. You have every right to be here. Allain would want you to be, wouldn't he? Not Francesca. You know that, so come on."

Betsy stood up, gave her friends a warm smile and walked into the ward. She stopped, took a deep breath and then walked on.

'Of course I should be here,' she told herself. 'I'm coming, Allain. I'm coming, my darling.'

After asking a nurse where she could find him, Betsy walked through the ward to a private room in the far corner. She got to the door, took another deep breath and opened it. There was total silence in the room, but Betsy noticed that nevertheless a group of people surrounded Allain's bed. As she opened the door all eyes turned to look at her. She stopped as they stared. Those who she supposed were Allain's family looked at her with expressions perplexed and questioning. Of course they did not know who she was. But another pair of eyes looked up at her, eyes burning full of hate and blazing with disbelief. It was a forbidding sight for Betsy, and she felt her courage and strength disappear. Then before she could go any further Francesca was out of her chair and at the door. She took Betsy roughly by the elbow and dragged her from the room.

"How dare you come here!" she hissed. "How dare you!"

With words barely audible, Betsy bravely replied, "But I love him. I had to come."

"Well, you can turn around and go home. We don't want you here. I can look after Allain. Just get out of his life. Go and don't come back."

She stormed back into the room and, breaking the peaceful

silence, she deliberately slammed the door in Betsy's face. For a few seconds Betsy stood hesitantly outside the door, wondering what she could do, but knowing she did not have the strength or the fortitude to go back in. In the few seconds she had been in the room she could only see Allain's bed surrounded by machines, tubes almost obliterating him from view. He seemed to be wrapped in coils and wires, his head just visible and immobile on the pillow. He may still have been alive, but at that moment Betsy felt she had lost him just as surely as if he was dead. How could she face the overwhelming love of his family group? No, they didn't need her; Allain didn't need her. Francesca was right: she should just go home.

Alderney no longer felt like home. It seemed an alien place. Betsy was bereft and, however hard she tried to be more positive, her future seemed so bleak. Indeed, she couldn't see any future for herself on Alderney, and it was only with difficulty that she could envisage any future at all. With Katy and Patrick gone, only Julie remained, and she couldn't and didn't even try too hard to persuade her to stay. There were only a few weeks of her contract at the bistro left, and she knew Julie could cope quite well without her. In the last few days even going out had been an effort. So many places on the small island brought back painful and at the same time bittersweet memories of the times she had spent with Allain. She couldn't even keep up to date with bulletins from the hospital. Julie was so kind and did this for her. The truth was that there was little or no improvement.

In the end it wasn't a hard decision to make: she was going home, home to Warwickshire. She would at least feel secure there, away from the memories and recent tragic events in her life. And what was more, she could try to forget the tragedy that had happened to Allain himself. After all, it was he, the lovely man, kind, generous, intelligent, with his life ahead of him, who had been dealt this dreadful blow. Even if he survived, what would his life be like? Betsy knew she shouldn't say it, but still life was so unfair.

'Allain didn't deserve this and I can't even help, not one little bit. What a coward I am,' she told herself. 'I'm running away – running back home to where I will be safe. Yet I don't know what else I can do!'

Betsy's heart leapt when she walked through the gate of her home. Autumn was in the air. The leaves on the trees were still green, yet many were falling gently – falling like confetti – as she walked slowly to the door, stopping sometimes to breathe in the air. It was a fine day, more cloud than blue sky but warm and clear. The front door was open before she even reached it and Jeannie came running out. Lovely Jeannie, who had looked after the house and Tom before she moved in. They hugged each other. Both had a tear in their eye, and Betsy could smell the familiar shampoo in Jeannie's hair and felt comforted and welcome.

"Yes, this is where I belong. At least here I can heal, surrounded by what is familiar, solid and permanent. I can feel safe here."

She walked on through the door to the drawing room, where Jeannie had already prepared tea and made scones, the aroma of which still permeated through from the kitchen.

On the sideboard she noticed flowers. 'Welcome Home' from Julie, and, from Katy and Patrick, roses: 'Good to have you back.'

She sat down by the fire, not necessary on the warm day, but welcoming as Jeannie knew it would be. She sipped the tea, sighed, sat back in her chair and inadvertently closed her eyes. A picture of Allain came into view, smiling, happy on the deck of his beautiful yacht. Tears pricked her eyes. Abigail, her cat, having long missed her 'mum', jumped on to her lap, purring loudly, face and fur brushing her neck. Her tears fell silently into Abigail's fur and the cat licked them gently away.

Life of course went on, and slowly over the weeks a semblance of a life reasserted itself for Betsy. She realised, as she never had for many months, how much she loved her home. Tom had bought Rowandean. His ancestral pile had long since become a literal pile and had been abandoned, most of the land sold. On his death the house and everything had passed to Betsy. Without children the title would be lost. Almost without realising it Betsy slipped into a peaceful, cocooned existence, gardening, walking, listening to music. It wasn't what she would have wished for herself, but she knew she was lucky to have this life to come back to.

On a crisp October morning Betsy was collecting apples when the telephone rang.

"Oh, hi, Katy. How are you?"

"I'm fine, Betsy – busy as hell at work, but I wanted to speak to you. I need to get you out into the real world again."

"Why? I'm fine too, really. What's wrong with my world?"

"The word 'hermit' comes to mind somehow. You never ring; I always ring you. Now listen, I've got tickets for the Shakespeare Theatre on Saturday. I'll pick you up at six. We'll have a pre-performance dinner."

"But—" Betsy tried to interrupt.

"No buts. I'll pick you up at six o'clock. Be ready."

"Yes, Sergeant," answered Betsy in mock anger, but she

was smiling. "I'd love to come. Thanks, Katy. See you Saturday."

'Life is moving on. This is a good place to be. I'm going to be all right. Yes, I'm sure of it.'

On the way back to her apples, Betsy had a spring in her step, and, for the first time for as long as she could remember, a song was humming in her head.

Chapter Ten

The telephone call came out of the blue.

"Hi, Julie. How are you? It's so lovely to hear from you."

And Betsy was genuinely pleased to hear from her. Julie had truly become a wonderful friend. Not that she phoned often, which was why Betsy was surprised and pleased to hear from her.

"And you, Betsy? How are you doing? You sound so much more cheerful. And thanks for the photographs. You have such a gorgeous house – I can visualise where you are now when I think of you."

"You must all come over and stay here. I owe you so much, and it would be great to see you again."

"We'd love to, but I'm not sure we can afford—"

"Don't worry about that – I'll pay for you."

"Betsy, that is so kind, but listen: I have a special reason for ringing."

Betsy suddenly felt a shiver run along her spine. 'This must be about Allain,' she said to herself. 'She's going to tell me he's dead.' Her knees went weak and she had to sit down.

"You've gone quiet, Betsy. Are you still there?"

"Yes, I'm here," she whispered.

"It's OK, Betsy, it isn't bad news. But it is about Allain."

"Oh!" was all she could muster.

"I need to tell you, but it's a long story. Are you listening?"

"Yes, Julie – go on," but not knowing whether or not she really did want to hear.

"Right, well, I had a phone call myself yesterday at the bistro. It's fortunate I was there. We are only opening short café hours as it goes so quiet in the autumn. Anyway, it was a hospital ward manager from a place called St Botolph's."

"Oh, where's that? I've never heard of it."

"No, nor had I, but it's actually in Southampton. It's a specialist unit and Allain was transferred there a week or so ago. Apparently he is still unconscious, but he is progressing and they think he will benefit from being there. But they are concerned because he is becoming very agitated. The manager said he is talking and shouting out, which is a good sign, she said."

"But why ring you, and at the bistro too?" Betsy asked, mystified but elated that Allain was improving.

"Well, that's the thing, Betsy," answered Julie. "It seems that what he is continually shouting is your name. The ward is very confused because they know that no one called Betsy has been to see him. They asked the family and friends if they knew anyone named Betsy and explained the situation. They said they had no idea why he was shouting the name; they said they did not know and never had known anyone at all called Betsy."

"Then Francesca must have lied – and deliberately too. How could she when she knew it was so important for Allain's recovery?"

By now Betsy felt herself growing hot and excited. Allain even subconsciously had not forgotten her. She knew she had to go and see him, and this time she was not going to be put off by the family, especially Francesca. She was stronger now – she was not going to be fobbed off.

"Oh, Julie, I can't believe all this. But how, then, did

they come to be able to contact you?"

"Well, it wasn't me they wanted, it was you. They decided to have a look through his things – with permission from his parents – and in his wallet was a card from the bistro with 'Betsy' written on it. So they rang the bistro, thinking you would still be there. They were so disappointed that you had left. Anyway, I asked if they would like me to contact you, and so here I am, talking to you now."

"Oh, Julie, how can I thank you!"

"You don't need to thank me; you need to get down to Southampton to see him. The doctors there really do think that if you are there it may well bring him out of the coma. His operations have been successful, and now he only needs to regain consciousness. If he does he may well make a complete recovery."

"I can't believe what you're telling me. It's more than I could ever have hoped. I thought I would never see him again. Of course I'll go straight away."

"You'll need to phone the hospital. Explain who you are and tell them that you are on the way."

"I will, I will. I'll do it now."

The ward staff told her to come, and having thrown some things into an overnight bag Betsy set off for Southampton. She didn't know the city at all, and it was a huge and busy place, but she found St Botolph's easily enough, a large new building with plenty of parking spaces. It was dusk as she arrived. A red sun dipping towards the horizon gave a golden glow where it glinted on the many panes of windows. It was cool and she walked briskly to the main entrance and stood by the bank of information boards to find the neurology ward. She took the lift to the second floor and saw the ward directly opposite when the lift doors opened. She felt a fluttering in her stomach, for while she desperately wanted to see and help Allain she was frightened too. How would he look? What would she say to him? What would the family say when they saw her? But undaunted she walked purposefully into the ward and up to the nurses' station, where Sister was busy with a telephone call. Betsy waited patiently, and when Sister finished her call she turned and smiled at Betsy.

"Sister Wells," Betsy began.

"Yes, can I help you?"

"I'm Betsy Abbot. I've come to see Allain Laubert."

"Oh, Betsy, how good of you to get here so soon. It's great you could come. We do hope your being here will help Allain. Would you like me to explain a few things for you and then you can go and see Allain?"

"That would be helpful, thank you."

Sister Wells took Betsy into a small room where they could speak privately. Betsy was relieved that someone was helping her to cope with the situation.

Ten minutes later, Betsy, feeling far more confident and with more information about what to expect, was taken to Allain's room, where Sister left her alone. She slowly pushed open the door, and felt her heart melt as she saw Allain lying still in his bed, eyes closed, pale and thin. There were still masses of tubes, but these didn't worry her. She knew they were keeping him alive. She took a chair from the side of the room, drew it to the bed and sat down quietly. She felt calm, but terribly sad.

"Oh, Allain; oh, my darling!"

And she took hold of his hand, which was limp, warm and dry. His eyes were closed, and his hand just lay in hers. No indication he knew she was holding it. It was so hard to comprehend that he was totally unconscious.

"What can I do for you, Allain? I love you so much. I

want you to get better. I won't leave – I'll stay here as long as I'm needed. I won't leave you again, I promise."

At first she was dismayed that there was no response at all, but it got easier and Betsy found herself simply talking about all sorts of things – the weather, her garden, Julie at the bistro. . . . When she ran out of things to say, she would rest a while and then start all over again.

No one said she had to leave, so when she started to feel tired, and noticed how late it was, she sat back in the chair and tried to sleep for a while. All the ward lights were switched off and Betsy felt herself drifting into a fitful sleep. It had, after all, been an exhausting day.

Suddenly Betsy felt herself jolted awake. It was dark and she was momentarily confused as to where she was and why. Then the hairs on the back of her neck started to rise and her skin pricked, for all she could hear was a distraught voice.

"Betsy, Betsy, where are you, Betsy? Why did you leave me, Betsy?"

Then there was quiet.

Then again: "Betsy, Betsy, I want Betsy."

After a few seconds Betsy realised that he was calling her from deep in his unconscious. Of course he didn't realise she was there.

She took his hand. "It's OK, Allain. It's me – Betsy. I'm here. I haven't left you. I'm here right beside you."

He became quiet. Betsy took a tissue and wiped his forehead, where in his agitation drops of perspiration lay glistening. Then she went to tell the nurses, who came to check on him.

"He's fine now. He's quiet, but it is a good sign. It means his brain is becoming more active and coming closer to the surface of consciousness."

Betsy dozed, and as dawn filtered through the curtains

she could hear the tea trolley moving along the ward and she was grateful when they brought her a cup of tea. And suddenly she felt hungry. When she looked at Allain he was calm and peaceful, and she decided to go down to the café for breakfast and then take some fresh air.

The rest of the day passed quietly. Betsy quickly became used to seeing Allain and was no longer shocked at his occasional outbursts. And she was determined to stay as long as she was needed, but she decided to stay at a hotel nearby for the night; she knew a good night's sleep would give her the strength and resilience she needed to help Allain. In the early evening she was sitting holding Allain's hand, talking low to Allain, explaining she was leaving but returning in the morning. She heard the door open and assumed it to be a nurse and didn't took up.

"What are you doing here?" a voice hissed at her. "How dare you come here! You have no right, do you hear! You have no right to be here. How did you find out where Allain was?"

Francesca was incandescent with rage, and before Betsy could even reply nurses swiftly approached perturbed by her loud, angry words.

"Please keep your voice down, Miss Duvall. What is the problem? You know this will not help your fiancé."

Betsy winced at the word, knowing that Francesca had no right to be calling herself such.

"The problem", replied Francesca in a very haughty manner, "is that I want this woman to leave. You must make her go. She has no right to be here, and I speak for Allain's family, who I know would want her barred from coming again."

"I'm afraid we can't do that. You'll have to take it up with Sister. Now perhaps you could come with us until you quieten down."

Now Betsy felt obliged to speak: "Actually, Francesca, I have every right to be here. In fact I was invited to come by the hospital. Allain's doctor thinks it will be beneficial to his healing for me to be here. And Allain's parents were aware that the hospital was making enquiries."

"Liar!" Francesca almost spat the words at her. "We'll see about that. I'm going to complain to the hospital. You won't get away with it."

Then she stormed out and slammed the door as she accompanied the nurses back on to the ward.

After she had gone, Betsy felt her composure leave her and she started to shake – not with fear or trepidation, but with purposeful determination. Finally she had stood up to Francesca. She did not know what would happen, but she knew she could cope with whatever it might be. Betsy now realised Allain needed her and she loved him. Nothing else mattered and no one was going to deflect her from her purpose. She felt strong and full of courage, and was determined to defend her rights whatever Allain's family and Francesca said or did.

Over the next few days Betsy fell into a kind of routine, but there were no significant changes or improvements. Allain's outbursts no longer disconcerted her and she patiently stroked his hand and his hair and spoke reassuringly to him. If his family came they carefully avoided her, and no doubt returned when Betsy had returned to her hotel for the night. Whatever the situation, there were no more angry encounters, for which Betsy was grateful.

She had also accepted the fact that maybe change was so slow as to be almost indiscernible. One afternoon of a grey, overcast, chilly day, she had returned to his bedside after stretching her legs and drinking a much needed coffee. The days could drag unmercifully and her little breaks were a necessary part of her day. She picked up a magazine and sat down by Allain's bed to read. It was only out of the corner of her eye that she thought she detected some movement, but then immediately dismissed it as imagination. Then she saw it again and knew it was real. It was fleeting, but Betsy was convinced he had moved his fingers. It was as if he momentarily reached for her hand. She took a sharp intake of breath and then called for the nurses. She was suddenly very excited.

"What is it, Betsy?" asked the nurses, who now had a cordial relationship with her.

"It's Allain. I'm sure he moved his fingers. He did – he definitely did."

"OK, OK, but let's not get too carried away. I don't want to disappoint you, but sometimes there can be some involuntary twitches from his muscles."

"No, it was more than that, really it was."

"Well, it could be significant. I'll get the Doctor to come and take a look."

When they had gone, Betsy began to doubt what she had seen. Allain looked just the same, peaceful and totally unaware.

"Oh, sweetheart, I really thought there was a change, but now I realise perhaps it was wishful thinking." She took his hand, squeezed it and then kissed him on his cheek. "Come on – it's me, Betsy. I need you so much. I love you more than anything in the world. I need you to get better. Fight – come on. Don't give up."

A tear fell on to his cheek. What more could she do? She felt helpless. It was so hard. She rested her head on her arms, which lay on the edge of the bed, and wept softly.

'Stop it,' she told herself. 'You said you were going to be strong. Now come on – bear up.' And she sat up, wiped her eyes and looked lovingly at Allain. 'If only he knew I was here.'

Then quite suddenly his eyelids flickered. Only briefly,

but she knew she wasn't mistaken this time. Then it happened again and she leapt up and rushed to the nurses' station to tell them what had happened.

This time everyone agreed it was significant. In fact, much more than that, they were even brave enough to suggest that Allain might even regain consciousness in the future. *Might*. Yes, that was the word – only *might* – but nevertheless Betsy was overjoyed, elated, and for the first time she believed there was hope.

Clearly it was significant because staff immediately contacted his family, who said they would fly over from Guernsey straight away. Betsy was determined to be discreet and make herself scarce. It was important for them – his parents needed to share in the new-found optimism. It was a good day – the first since she had arrived.

'Thank You, Lord, and thank You for giving me the strength to cope."

For the next couple of days there were no further changes or improvements, though the flickering eyelids and twitchy fingers continued and helped maintain Betsy's optimism. Yet her optimism became tempered with fatigue and worry, and she had to check herself when she found thoughts like 'Could this be all the improvement we will see?' creeping into her mind. She was lonely too. It was hard to be continually upbeat when she had no one to talk to; the nurses and doctors were kind and reassuring, but they were busy and had many other patients and their families to attend to.

Then one evening as she was about to leave she saw two people approaching Allain's room. Although she had never met them she knew instinctively that they were Allain's parents. As they came through the door Betsy stood up to leave. She was embarrassed, disconcerted, not knowing what she should do.

Allain's mother was obviously aware of Betsy's discomfort because she immediately addressed her: "No, don't leave, Betsy. You are Betsy, aren't you?"

"I am."

"Please sit down again. We knew you would be here – we don't want you to leave."

"But I don't understand," answered a flummoxed Betsy.

This time it was Allain's father who spoke: "We thought it was about time we met you. Of course we didn't know about you before, and when the doctors asked us about you we genuinely couldn't help. Francesca didn't tell us, you see. It was only when the staff here explained that we understood you were a real person."

"At first", continued Mrs Laubert, who sat down beside Betsy when her husband brought over two chairs, "we didn't know what to think. We didn't know who you were or where you figured in Allain's life. We have realised since that you were clearly very important to each other, and we accepted the Doctor's opinion that you could be crucial to Allain's recovery."

"We want you to know", Mr Laubert said, "that we are glad you are here, and we want to thank you for being here for him."

Betsy's eyes filled with tears – tears of relief and gratitude that she had been accepted and was no longer isolated and alone.

"I love him," she replied. "I'll stay as long as he needs me. I'm so happy to meet you at last." And she smiled through her tears.

"So shall we join you and see what Allain has been up to today?"

"Oh yes, I would like that. It has been so lonely on my own."

"That's settled, then. Perhaps we should introduce

ourselves properly," said Allain's mother. "I'm Elizabeth and this is my husband, Robert."

"And I am Betsy Abbot, from Warwickshire and lately Alderney, where Allain and I met."

So time passed, but better times. Betsy was coping better now with support from Allain's parents, but it was nevertheless worrying and stressful for them all.

One evening after a day when Allain had been more agitated than usual, Betsy decided to stay with him for the night, hoping her words would comfort and compose him. As the night wore on Betsy found her head drooping, falling on to her hands, which were resting on the bed. She felt exhausted and fell asleep.

As had happened at other times when she had inadvertently fallen asleep, she was wakened with a jump. The first she knew she felt a hand moving beneath her and knew immediately it was Allain and he was moving, without any doubt. She gasped, opened her eyes, switched on his bedside light and turned to look at him. In total shock she saw that Allain's eyes were open, *open*, moving and blinking.

"Oh my God, Allain, you're awake! Can you hear me? Can you see me? Allain, Allain, oh, my darling!"

She pressed the button for the Nurse and she came immediately. It was readily apparent that this truly was a miraculous moment.

"He's opened his eyes, Nurse. He has opened his eyes."

And she went over to him, kissed his forehead and then moved away while the nurse approached.

"Is he conscious? Can he see or hear?"

"We don't know yet," the Nurse answered, "but the signs are good – very good indeed."

Betsy sat down, relief and happiness flooding through her. She put her hand on his, stroked and kissed it and then the most wonderful thing of all was she felt his hand move and he grasped her fingers and whispered, "Betsy."

"I think that is our answer, Betsy. I'd say yes, he's conscious," said a delighted nurse.

It was more than Betsy had dared hope, but Allain was indeed conscious, and more than that he was aware. As the days and his recovery progressed it was obvious too that there was no brain damage. In fact his recovery was so rapid and so conclusive that within a couple of weeks he was allowed home.

"I never thought I would ever see this, Allain," Betsy said as she escorted him in his wheelchair to his parents' car.

"But it's all due to you, Betsy," Allain answered. "I was waiting for you and I know it was your voice which woke me up."

She kissed the top of his head. "Now come on – here's your dad to help you in."

"You won't stay away long, will you, Betsy?" he appealed.

"No, sweetheart. I'm just dashing back to Warwickshire, then I'll be on Guernsey in no time. I'm not leaving you again in a hurry."

"You can stay with us for as long as you wish, Betsy," Elizabeth said.

"Thank you," said Betsy and gave Elizabeth a hug. Then she went to Allain in the car. "And I'll see you very soon. Have a safe journey. Love you."

"Love you too." And they both kissed.

"See you shortly, then," shouted Robert through the car window as they drove off.

Betsy waved until they had completely disappeared, off to the ferry, next stop Guernsey.

Time sped by. Christmas came and went, and Betsy, staying at the Laubert house, watched as Allain recuperated and gained strength and confidence. Their love grew also and they were both now brave enough to look forward to see a future for themselves – something which only six months before she could never have imagined. Of Francesca there was no sign. She never visited or telephoned – at least not to Betsy's knowledge. Neither Allain's parents nor Allain himself ever mentioned her, and so nor did Betsy.

Guernsey very rarely sees snow, but despite its mild climate winter can still be cold. One crisp February morning, a clear day of sparkling blue sky and winter sunshine, Allain's doctor visited and said he felt Allain was fit enough to go back to his own home and go back to work. Betsy, who had been out shopping, missed his visit but was delighted with the news.

"Betsy, come here," Allain said. "I can't believe we have all come through this. And what's more I didn't realise how much you loved me, that you could go through it all with me." He stretched out, took her hands and pulled her to him. "It may not be the most romantic of situations, but it is Valentine's Day. Betsy Abbot, I love you more than anything or anyone in the whole world. Will you marry me?"

"I will, I will, Allain. I love you so much, I can't imagine being anywhere but with you, forever."

Allain drew her to him and gave her the longest, most passionate kiss she had ever known. It truly was a beautiful day.

Chapter Eleven

They were married on Alderney at St Anne's Church. Betsy looked stunning in an ice-blue silk dress with a bouquet of blue hyacinths and jonquils, while Allain matched her brilliantly in his pale-blue waistcoat and pale-lemon tie. Betsy couldn't believe she could be so lucky, and Allain too knew he was lucky in many ways. He still wasn't back to full health, but he knew it would come with time. Outside the church it was a beautiful late spring day with a blue sky and a slight breeze. The small reception would be at the yacht club, and so they decided to walk down the street with all their family and friends to the harbour and enjoy the sunshine on the way.

As they strolled down the street well-wishers and visitors alike gathered to watch the little party and clapped and cheered as they walked by. It was so wonderful and more than she could have ever expected. There were further photographs down by the harbour, and when they finally arrived at the yacht club a small welcoming party of fellow yachtsmen waited outside holding flags aloft and forming an arch for them to pass under.

When the magical day and evening had passed, Betsy and Allain had only a couple of hundred yards to walk to the jetty where they were to spend their honeymoon night on the *Jonquil*.

The *Jonquil*: Betsy had never even wondered what had happened to her. Allain had told her that after the accident she was badly damaged in the storm and had been towed in. Allain's father had had her repaired and here she was like new, bobbing gently in the water, waves lapping and slapping against the jetty. She was waiting and welcomed them.

"Come on," Allain said, "be careful, it's a bit slippery," as he helped her on board.

They both stood on the small deck and looked up at the sky and then at each other.

"Thank you," said Betsy.

"What for?" Allain questioned.

"For a wonderful day, for loving me and wanting to marry me."

"Oh, Betsy, I love you so much and you know we might never have had this chance."

"No, we must never forget how near we were to losing each other. We have so much to be grateful for."

And as they stood together in the balmy spring night they watched the myriad of stars, and from behind a small cloud emerged a perfect full moon. The moon sent moonbeams down on to the water, which glowed in the night air. It was magical. Could she ever want more than this? Betsy asked herself. 'No, never' came the answer. She put her arms around Allain's neck, her eyes glistening with tears.

"I love you."

And she kissed him long and lovingly with happiness and wonder that she could be so happy.

Then suddenly there was a commotion further along the quay, laughter and footsteps. As they approached, Betsy and Allain could see familiar faces; all their family and friends had followed them down.

"You didn't think you could get away that easily, did

you?" shouted Katy. "We've got champagne for us and to rechristen the boat."

Allain and Betsy laughed heartily.

"Come on board – if you can all get on, that is," shouted Allain.

And it was indeed a tight squeeze, but everyone managed it, the celebrations continuing until the early hours.

It was a bleary-eyed but elated couple who sailed off soon after dawn on the calm and almost windless tide for their short honeymoon.

"Where are you taking me, then, sweetheart?" enquired Betsy, who was still in the dark as to their ultimate destination.

"Wait and see. We'll be there in a few hours – you won't have long to wait. But honestly, Betsy, do you really not mind us having such a short honeymoon? I missed so much work during my illness, I'll have to make it up somehow."

"I know, and how many times have I told you that, no, of course it doesn't matter? Just a couple of days relaxing together will be great."

They lapsed into an easy silence, and enjoyed an almost perfect sail, and later Betsy watched as land approached. She knew it was France, but where exactly she wasn't sure.

"St Malo," announced Allain as they approached the mouth of the harbour. "It's a beautiful place and we can then sail further up the coast. There's somewhere else I really want to take you. I know you'll like it."

That place was Deauville, where Allain was determined to let Betsy see the place where her grandfather and other ancestors had lived.

Yes, it had been short, but it was a perfect honeymoon none the less, and as they sailed leisurely back to St Peter Port Betsy was relaxed and glowing from the sea air and all her unexpected experiences. The *Jonquil* seemed pleased to be back in her usual mooring and, when she was secured,

Betsy and Allain jumped off knowing they were about to begin their new lives together.

"I'll come back for our things later. We've plenty of time," Allain said.

They walked hand in hand along the pontoon and then continued on to the main walkways, Betsy pointing to Allain's apartment (now their home) on the waterfront.

"Oh, Betsy, look at the big liner moored up. Looks fabulous. I wonder where she's going from here. Somewhere very nice, I imagine."

"Look – she's the *Queen Mary*!" exclaimed Betsy as they drew closer. "How long will she stay here?"

"Just today, I imagine. She will probably have moored up last night, and the passengers will be spending the day in St Peter Port. We get a lot of cruise ships these days. Probably she'll sail this evening. I wonder if we could find out where she's off to?" asked Allain.

"I don't know, but we can go and see if any of the crew can tell us. Come on," encouraged Betsy.

The ship was so tall and she towered over them.

"I can't see how we'll see any crew – they'll never see us or hear us. Never mind, it was just a thought." But Betsy was disappointed.

"Oh, hold on, Betsy. Look – there's someone coming down the passenger gangway."

They approached him.

"Are you waiting to see people off? You'll have a long wait if you are – we don't sail until this evening," said the crewman.

"Oh, no, we were just admiring the ship. I haven't seen the *Queen Mary* before."

"She's certainly a beautiful ship. Would you like to come and have a look around?"

"Oh, I don't know," Betsy replied. "It seems rude somehow."

"No, honestly, you're welcome. You aren't the first to want to admire her."

"What do you think, Allain?"

"I think if we've been invited then we should gratefully accept."

"OK, then, we will."

And off they went, following the crewman up on to the vast deck. They were left to look around.

"He's very trusting, isn't he, letting us look on our own?"

"We must look honest, but I think he's probably busy too."

"You're right. She's gorgeous, isn't she? But he never did tell us where she was sailing to."

"No, he didn't, did he?"

"Oh, Allain, I can see all the passengers walking towards the ship."

"It must be time for them to board. Perhaps they are having dinner in port before sailing."

Passengers started to stream up on to the deck.

"I think we'd better go, don't you?"

"Yes, come on," agreed Allain, and they walked along the deck and waited for passengers to board, hoping for a gap so they could disembark.

Then the same crewman appeared.

"Hello again. What do you think, then?"

"I think she's gorgeous, but we need to be leaving. Thank you for letting us on board. It's been great."

"But why are you leaving? Your cabin is this way – isn't that right, Allain?"

"Yes, that's right, Keith."

He looked at Betsy, who was thoroughly perplexed as she looked from one to the other. Allain's eyes shone with amusement.

"Do you mean we are sailing on the *Queen Mary*?"

said Betsy in wonderment. "But I haven't any luggage or anything. You're having me on."

"Would I do that? Betsy, your luggage is already on board, and there's champagne waiting in our suite. So would you care to join me?"

And Allain took Betsy's hand and led her away. She was beaming from ear to ear.

"What a dark horse! I can't believe you organised all this and kept it quiet."

"Well, I did. You didn't really think I wouldn't organise a proper honeymoon, did you?"

"Oh, Allain, I love you."

"Well, come on, Mrs Laubert – the champagne will be warm if we don't hurry, and when we've drunk it I'll tell you where we sail to next. You see, I've known all the time."